# TOWARDS THE SOUND

# TOWARDS THE SOUND

*Understanding Our Origins*

**Suryansh Shekhar**

*Published by*
**PRABHAT PRAKASHAN PVT. LTD.**
4/19 Asaf Ali Road,
New Delhi-110 002 (INDIA)
e-mail: prabhatbooks@gmail.com

ISBN 978-93-5521-761-5
**Towards the Sound**
*by* Shri Suryansh Shekhar



*Edition*
First, 2023

*Price*
₹ 250.00 (Rupees Two Hundred Fifty only)

*Printed at*
R-Tech Offset Printers, Delhi

# About the Author

Suryansh Shekhar is a philosophical seer, singer, guitarist and actor that worked with the National School of Drama as a child and astounded everyone at the 'Bharat Rang Mahotsava' by playing the lead in the 3 hour long play 'Purana Ghar' by Shekhar Joshi. Suryansh is also a Director and Sound Engineer who has worked on International Award winning Films 'Pimpal' and 'Sohala' with National Award winning Director Gajendra Ahire and prominent film maker K.C. Bokadia. He belongs to a generation of writers as he is the grandson of Padmabhushan Pt. Suryanarayan Vyas and the son of prominent hindi writer Raj Shekhar Vyas.

Despite all this, he is a young solitaire ascetic at his core. He has managed to encompass the crux of the 'Vedas,' 'Puranas' and the 'Upanishads' along with 'The Gita,' 'Ramayan' and 'The Mahabharata,' in his first writing. He is no scholar in the field of English writing yet his piece reads like a flowing river.

A prominent scholar suggested that after a

reading of this book, one can easily sense the echoes of the likes of Maharishi Raman, Arvind, Vivekananda or Rajneesh and that the book encapsulates their thought in such a manner that a known scholar of these areas would enjoy it even more.

The book speaks on Purpose, Meaning, Sorrow, Pleasure, Fear, Societal Pressure and other things that stem from ancient wisdom. From Bertrand Russell, Albert Einstein, Khalil Gibran to Kundanika Kapadia, all find their voices resonating in this piece.

This book is a treasure for the youth that often ends up being a misguided victim of parental and social pressure. The book can be revisited multiple times and opens newer dimensions with every read. It is without a doubt, an essential for the current generation.

**—Kumar Yogi**
(Writer)

# REVIEWS

## Facing Towards the Sound

Suryansh Shekhar has the makings of a genius. His book 'Towards the Sound' traces the wonderful journey of how a man reviews his brain and tunes his frequency to the eternal sound.

This is a book that brings the Universe to light, literally. It puts a human face and heart on the Universe. The book shows his passion and commitment with guts, tenacity and verve. A well written book with challenging and interesting inter weaving of science and present spiritual/mystical concepts.

Towards the Sound is a classic of modern spirituality based cosmology. Cosmic evolution is a multi-level self organisation that includes physical, chemical, biological, cultural and technological evolution. The book talks about how we are the manifestation of a single evolutionary process. Whilst reading the book you will find yourself experiencing a sense of wonder at the sheer beauty of deep space.

It is an amazing narrative with an easy style

and immanent flow. The underlying message that it resonates with is surely worth a read.

**—Kaveri Mukherji**
Journalist
(Ex. BBC & Doordarshan)

## A Homage to the 'Self'

Self awareness is the capacity to look inward and understand our own feelings, emotions, stresses and personality. This key understanding plays a critical role in influencing our judgement, decision and interaction with other people. Suryansh Shekhar's 'Towards the Sound' is a gentle nudge towards understanding the construct of self and link between inner and outer world and how these identities are constructed.

It is reassuring to find Suryansh centre staging an important subject with such great sensitivity, purpose and awareness. Suryansh's prose makes what might otherwise be a challenging topic, engaging and relatable. A wonderfully thoughtful book for everyone to reflect upon.

**—Rehan Fazl**
Journalist (BBC)

# The Author's Lens

Suryansh is a young man who clearly likes to think deeply. He analyses persons and situations and their interactions, attempting to try and articulate motivations, separating those that are innate to a person's essential being and those that emanate from the surrounding material and social universe.

He is a seeker, as evidenced in his writing, and he wants his readers to also delve into self-analysis to arrive at a more considered and meaningful approach to the world around them, leading to a more centered existence, in harmony with the 'true' self. This is truly commendable in one as young as he is and he has managed to shed light on a truly mature concept.

**—Sunit Tandon**
Art Critic & Theatre Personality

# Mysteries of the Soul

It goes without saying that knowing yourself is the beginning of all wisdom. Who in the world am I? We do not dare to ask this question to ourselves. Why? Perhaps, we are afraid that the answer might not be of our liking. However, your visions will become clear only when you can look into your own heart. Surely, you can't lie to your soul. The more powerful and original a mind, the more it will incline towards the religion of solitude.

In his inaugural book, young author Suryansh Shekhar tries to answers some of these questions. "Who are we? Are we just observers watching our selves commit actions and do what we just skate through our lives on the sidelines or are we the ones committing those actions," he asks.

An introspective person is someone who regularly looks inward to try to understand his mind, thoughts, feelings, and inner workings. He might engage in meditation or other contemplative practices. He might just pause to self-reflect when something is bothering him, when he handled a situation poorly, or when he is just curious to learn more about himself.

It is said that the unexamined life is not worth living. While this dictum is true, self-reflection is not an easy thing to practice. As we live in an incredibly fast-paced world, our mobile phones are constantly buzzing, social media is infinitely calling, and Netflix always has something new to binge on. Taking the time for reflection is a bit of a lost art. Most of us, unfortunately, are living unexamined lives.

While we often discuss the traits of our friends and family members, we hardly spare time for the introspection of our self. Introspection is one of the qualities of a mature person and despite being so young, Suryansh Shekhar has discussed the subject deftly and with tremendous amount of authority.

You would not meet many people who often try to find the answers to questions like: "What is my purpose in life?", "What is the real meaning of 'Satisfaction'?" or "What exactly is 'boredom'?" While we have been trying to find the real meaning of all these issues, we remain unsatisfied with the conclusions that we draw from our own experiences. We always feel that what we are thinking is perhaps not correct or complete. You would agree with me that it is a question as old as time: "What is my purpose in life?"

As far back as the fourth century BC, Aristotle was keenly thinking about life's purpose. In today's fast-paced, technology-filled world where we are being pulled in many directions at once, finding the purpose of life seems more important than ever. We meet people spending their lives reacting to situations instead of being proactive and figuring out the needs and values that drive them. As that is not enough, when they think they know their purpose, they often mistake it with a short-term goal. Many people are also asking themselves the question of purpose in life but they have no idea how to find it.

As he says, "It is a natural human instinct to believe that there must be a reason for everything. While science is busy answering the 'whats' behind the little known facts of the universe, religion is attempting to answer the 'whys.' Religion is actually built on that attempt and that is why we have so many religious people in the world because we desperately need a reason or a purpose behind things... So then, what is our purpose? Why are we here? We are certainly not here for a 9 to 5 job. That is not to say that one shouldn't have a job. However, could it really be all that we are here for?"

Young thinker Suryansh tries to unlock the mysteries of all these questions and more, at a length and while going through this book, you would find some amazing thoughts that would give you enough fodder to think in a different perspective. The book gives an idea that he has arrived as an accomplished author and one only hopes that his journey as a writer would go a long way in dealing with questions in respect of 'The self.'

**—Vivek Shukla**

Journalist (Times of India)

# Preface

Life, as a cliché goes, is a journey. However, it is an unpredictable journey that has, besides joy, phases riddled with uncertainty, anxiety and fear about what the future has in store. Anxieties may be *qua* teachers, friends, parents, relationships, co-workers or public discourse in general. When anxious and fearful, many withdraw into their shells, and, worse, become dysfunctional.

Those living in the present 'age of information,' while blessed with material comforts that were made widely available by the preceding industrial age, are facing an unprecedented challenge of humungous proportions: mental distress. Unlike ever before, in this information technology age, human minds are being invaded from varied directions by facts, half-truths, falsehoods and unbaked wisdom. It is difficult to talk just about anything with certitude. Anecdotal evidence, and indeed researched publications, suggest that compared to any previous generation, the mind space of today's youth is witnessing far more intense battles between contrasting ideas and social pressures. The battles waging within individual minds, riddled with anxiety and fear, can no longer be taken lightly—neither by young nor by their parents and well-wishers.

Suryansh Shekhar, the author of this book, all of 30 years, grew up in cosmopolitan New Delhi. He has worked in corporate sector, publishing houses and is engaged in artistic pursuits in Mumbai as well. He has stepped forward to give us an understanding of anxiety and how to cope with it. This young man's journey into his mind, it appears, had its tortuous turns. Looking within, he says, can lead to clarity and calmness.

In dealing with anxiety and stress, Suryansh has, by way of examples, given a glimpse of factors contributing to anxiety, for this generation. He has swiftly traversed to matters of wider interest to suggest that dilemmas and anxieties are best addressed by 'going within.' The author has shared a journey towards attaining calmness.

The book in your hand—a collection of essays by a sensitive soul coping with the world around him—may motivate you to pause to reflect on your anxieties and the need to address them.

The author's ruminations on the themes addressed, will, hopefully, help the readers in their respective onward journeys.

**—Raman Nanda**
Journalist (Ex BBC)
Jaipur, January 2023

# An Introduction

What is an introduction? When we meet someone new then we are introduced to him/her. When someone introduces a new person to us then he/she tells us something about that new person. With that Introduction we form a first impression of that person. We perceive him/her in a certain manner and form an image of him/her in our minds.

Now, the truth is that no matter what we perceive about him/her, an introduction never creates a complete picture of who he/she is. We can never know that person completely based on an introduction. A first impression might attract us or repel us from that person's personality but it is never a complete picture. You may end up liking someone in the long run whose first impression was not attractive and at the same time someone who really clicked with you on the first impression may not be a likable person in the long run. First impressions are never a complete black or white, it is a grey where your judgement of that person is responsible for drawing the image of him. So an introduction to anything can only partly paint the picture of that entity and sadly based on that you decide whether you want to indulge into that entity any further.

This book longs for an introduction that can completely paint a legitimate picture of what you are about to read. 'Towards the sound' not only speaks of the human journey towards the eternal lasting sound but it also represents nature's journey towards a sound mind. It is a movement towards understanding our origins and gradually getting used to looking at life in a more objective manner. It showcases a movement through the various structures of social realms to give you an understanding of the world around you, the ability to deal with it and in due course help you reach an unconquerable, soundness of the mind. However, the truth is that an introduction will never suffice and would only give you a partial picture of what all lies within this book and the attempt would still be to give you something that is close to the complete image.

This book practically wrote itself and has very little to do with the author on a personal level. The author is merely a tool that the book uses to express itself. Every chapter in the book has a different identity and they can all be treated as separate from each other, while at the same time the book has been divided into three sections that give the entire piece a certain unity in a sense.

The three sections are closely interlinked and talk about different walks of life where we as humans struggle. The first section, 'On Nature', talks about how things are within the nature of the human mind and the battle of the mind to survive within the given circumstances of its essential nature. The second section, 'On Society,' talks about the influence of society on our 'self' and how the struggle for survival within that domain is. The third section 'On Being' sheds light on the aspects of our own emotions that end up creating a struggle to survive within the world. All three sections gradually explain the tact to deal with these struggles and focus on creating a 'sound' mind that is capable of dealing with all the battles that life has to offer.

The first section focuses on opening new doors of 'perception' and helps us develop an understanding of how most of our problems arise from how we perceive things. It helps us understand that there is an other side to things and when we begin to view things objectively we can realise our full potential as a person. It essentially suggests that the noise that 'the matrix' of the world pumps in our heads can gradually be overcome when we begin to see it for the noise that it is.

The second section focuses on dealing with all kinds of people and circumstances. It encourages the willingness to meet and understand new people. It speaks of a social evolution over a technological one. It speaks of a generation that has completely misunderstood each other and is constantly in a battle where judgement of each other's choices prevails. The answer to which lies in understanding that we are all in a collective journey of evolution, where nature is trying to make sense of itself and the movement longs a rediscovering of communication.

The final section is a longer one and it speaks of

all that is needed to develop a sound mind. It develops in us, the capacity to understand all walks of life and give equal importance to them. Along with that, it focuses on developing a certain fluidity of character which enables one to easily dissolve into situations. This section essentially is about how one works on their 'self' and gradually paves way to becoming a complete personality that can conquer all the battles of life.

In conclusion, the only thing that can be said about this book is that it is less complicated than it seems and is a light read. It only envisions to lead you to eternal peace and provide you with all the tools required to make life an easy ride.

□

# Contents

# ON NATURE

## *Chapter 1*

# Magnetism and the Sense of Self

Before we begin, the rudimentary question we must ask ourselves is "Who are we?" Are we just observers watching our selves commit actions and do we just skate through our lives on the sidelines or are we the ones committing those actions? Is not our self a finely crafted image of who we want to be or want to be seen as in the presence of the society around us, so that we fit in with all others and are seen as normal functioning humans that adhere to the norms, conventions and expectations set by society? In fact, is not society as a majority, moving towards some collective understanding of trend and times and in turn becoming how we want to be seen? Are we free to make choices beyond these norms or does the pressure of society simply restrict our paths to certain limited directions? Before we get into what society does to us, let us first address the nature of how things are. So, who are we?

We are who we've become in our journey through time and eventually, without realising we end up becoming who we think we are. We've heard the phrase plenty of times that the world is a stage and we are mere characters playing our respective roles. This isn't far from the truth because what we consider real or natural is also a pretense which is so finely crafted or is a role played with such conviction that it appears to be real. So what is left of us, if all is pretense? We shall get into that gradually but in a broad sense what is left is the sense of self.

The self can easily be confused with our actions, behavior or who we've become through time. However, it is the essence of our being. Most people use meditative practices in order to find their true selves. People read through stoic wisdom in search of their inner selves. The search of self is not a new concept and we shall try and get into it with as much ease as possible.

Every little interaction that we have with the universe has an impact on our selves and it transforms us into something different from who we really are. Say, you are listening to a song that is slow paced and packed with emotion, this song can remind you of a memory and make you cry. A song with an upbeat feel can put you in a joyous mood. Essentially what is happening here is that your mind is adapting to the interaction that it had with the universe in the form of a song. It is merely a response to stimulus.

In the same way when you meet a person, his demeanor and behavior has an impact on yours and you adapt and behave in the way that the situation demands of you. Which also means that you are not who you are in that moment but rather you are a mix of how you want that person to see you and how that person actually sees you. You slowly become a response to the stimulus of the people around you. There is a certain behavior expected from you in every situation and that essentially transforms you into who you become based on where you are. So defining your space and giving time to yourself is essential for you to keep your true self intact or you might end up losing yourself completely into who you've become. Let us now address this 'who we've become' in the meanwhile so we can systematically deconstruct this constructed self which we would call Default Mode Network or DMN.

Think about driving a car with manual transmission. You're shifting gears, maintaining your speed limit, applying breaks at the right time, angling your steering wheel and coordinating with the traffic around you. You're using your mind for this tumultuous multi-task to quite an extent, the processing speed of which is almost unimaginable. However, you're not really consciously thinking about any of these tasks while you are performing them. It occurs naturally and is now a part of your system in the DMN. So most things enter our mind through our conscious selves and eventually become a natural instinct. Though these instincts are not who we are, it is merely who we've become to adapt to our environments.

Similarly, when we have a natural response to every little interaction with people and things we end up thinking that it is who we are and we hardly ever stop to think that maybe this isn't ourselves. There is no sense of self in these moments. To actually take out the time to find ourselves seems useless when life is flowing smoothly.

If we look at this from the beginning, as children we adapted to our environment and began to acquire tastes sometimes guided by rationale or wisdom which majorly stemmed from the influence of either a person or generally the society around us. So in that sense our DMN, this perfect actor on the world stage or what we've become, this "who we think we are" is a mere composite of acquired tastes. We delude ourselves to believe that it is who we are, not just out of unawareness but because it settles into our environment with such perfection that most people remain their constructed selves throughout their lives because it helps them drive their cars with ease and much convenience.

Now, if we are just this composite of acquired tastes or these constructions, so to say, then that also means that we can be freer than before because what we never liked before or always had a repulsion to can now be looked at with an open mind and can be a taste that we can acquire. At the same time, everything unnecessary that you chose to accept as a consequence of society's influence that you have now gotten fond of, can be systematically discarded and you can make space for newer tastes. Think of it like those magnets that reverse their force when turned. This opening of your mind and this ability to view things differently isn't that far away once you know who you are not. So, what you eat, what music you listen to, who you meet, the time you sleep, the profession you're in and all your tastes are susceptible to change when you understand the mechanism behind every force that pulls or pushes you.

Every entity has its own magnetic force and it is constantly pushing and pulling you in a certain direction. This magnetism works both ways. What you attract and repel is also a factor and you pull and push things too. The trees, beautiful rivers, people and objects are all there in an attempt to interact with you. What you push away or get pulled into is completely your choice if you look at it that way. You are free in every sense and can be unphased by the magnetic force of things and people around you. All you need is to have the willingness to turn your magnet in the direction you want.

Your response to every interaction can be more confident when you are not constantly seeking approval from everyone you meet. We mostly are constantly transforming ourselves to suit someone else's preferences. We are often too concerned about how someone else perceives us and we naturally move from 'who we are' to 'who we want to be seen as'. When you use rationale to restrict yourself from a real interaction then not only are you depriving your self from having the joy of living but what you feel about that interaction is also just your perception. You have assumed how you would appear to a person and all that you are, is lost in the process. The irony is that maybe what you think you are appearing to be like, may also not be perceived in the way you want by that someone. So here you are playing your character with conviction and yet are misinterpreted and in this entire pretense you never get to be yourself either.

You're mostly concerned with the fact that maybe you won't be likable if you simply be yourself and this is sadly, all in your head.

In the magnetic sense of it you are literally repelling yourself from this person without realising it and in the process depriving your inner self the joy of living. You are free to be yourself yet you use rationale to put across a version of yourself that according to you fits the social circumstance. This is the reason why a majority of the people are fake and are constantly smothering their 'selves' without realising it. The reason behind this entire charade is that we as humans fear judgement. As long as that fear exists we can never truly live even after finding our inner selves. What someone else thinks of us should never be the initial concern before entering into any interaction. The initial concern should be understanding the other person's perspective so that the interaction can be a real one.

If you are willing to change your perspective about a certain entity and open your mind, you will not only realise that there is much more to all that you see and believe, but you will also soon begin to feel the attraction and repulsion you emit towards objects and people. This magnetism that we speak of is also constantly shaping you and molding you with every little interaction you have with the outside world, as you consciously make an effort to be the way you want to be seen as. With an open mind not only can you change the way you see things and people but also how you see yourself. Your focus will shift from 'how you want to be seen as' to 'how you see things and people'. You will stop being an inward personality and will begin to develop newer perspectives on things and people. You will feel a certain warmth in the way you approach life altogether.

Your self can only truly be found when you are completely immersed into the feeling of being with your own self. You need to stop, think and observe its immanent flow. Though these magnetic forces are all around us all the time, yet a confident self that is aware of its existence is unaffected by these forces of the universe. The only way to feel this power within ourselves is, when once you have had a sense of its existence, you begin to give time to your self. You need to feel its presence and understand the silence and serenity it brings with itself. It watches you play these social games and never complains. Its dormancy holds a fearless volcano of creativity and confidence. All it needs is to be heard.

With the awareness of its existence comes a calmness in character and your nature becomes more like water. You take the shape of the vessel you're put in and when a stone is thrown at you it ends up sinking with ease and without much turbulence. Things and people then begin to align themselves to your frequency because it is calm yet immovable in its essence. They may try to bring out a version of you that they want to see but your warmth soon begins to attract them and they slowly settle in like stones in water.

The truth is that your 'self' was unaware of its own existence as a separate entity. It practically never even existed because it was busy playing its role with conviction, adapting to its environment in order to survive. This constructed self is also finely crafted and beautiful. It cannot be discarded completely. In most social situations it turns out to be your savior. In fact, you can always choose to remain your former self but life isn't a car to be driven subconsciously in a Default Mode while you're sitting in the passenger seat. It is your car and you should get to feel the joy of driving it too.

□

*Chapter 2*

# Quantum Entanglement and the Question of Choice

Now, What is choice really? Do we even have any or what we get is a mere illusion of choice? Is it even possible to break these illusions that are built by our surroundings, conditioning and a whole network of thoughts, ideas, rationale, norms and wisdom that have not only shaped us from the very beginning but also govern the laws of the world around us? Are we willing to rebel against all this and are we not afraid of being abandoned by everything around us? Are we not so dependent on the structure that escaping it is mere fantasy and can rarely be transitioned into reality?

Our actions are majorly dependent on two things, the taste we've acquired over the years and our environment or circumstances. In essence, it is a combination of the things we want to do and the things available to us within our circumstances. Which means say you want to watch your favorite TV show, that is your taste, it defines who you are. Now, say you have all the resources to watch it, an internet connection, a TV or a laptop, a house, spare time and your family's approval. These are the resources available in your environment to enable you to pursue your interest/taste.

Now, say around the time you planned to watch that TV show, a friend comes in and wants to take you out for lunch and at the same time your mother is sitting in the sun relaxing. You could choose to sit in the sun with your mother or go out for lunch and interact with your friend but your DMN won't let you choose anything else. Quantum Entanglement, in essence suggests that sometimes an interaction of one particle with the other is linked to such an extent that their state remains the same regardless of the distance between them. It is like an unbreakable bond. So while you would end up believing that you made a choice, the truth is you never had one.

There is nothing wrong in pursuing your taste and using resources, we are not looking at this action with critical scrutiny. The issue at hand is the fact that there was so much more available in terms of resources within that same environment which could have helped us explore other dimensions to our environment, which we ignored because our taste took priority. This constructed self has been hardened by years of authority over your mind and to break through that shell is never an easy task. It takes what it wants and will explore no further and offer you a rational justification that would seem acceptable because of which the doors to your mind remain shut to the vast universe outside.

The DMN will have many reasons to convince you

why watching the show is justified. Maybe going out with your friend is just a waste of time and maybe sitting in the sun with your mother will not be as productive either. However, what we don't realise is that doing so would still be considered a step towards opening your mind to exploration of newer tastes and rewiring your brain.

This works the same in every domain of life. Even something as serious as a 'choice of profession' works on the same principles. Your conditioning or the taste you've acquired over the years along with the available options within your environment or your circumstance is essentially also responsible for who you become in terms of profession.

Say, you've just graduated from high school and chosen to be an engineer. Let us not even get into family pressure and a societal push in that direction that actually landed you in that field. Let us leave aside assumptions like how your father was in the same field and inspired you as a child to be in the same profession. Let us simply assume you have acquired a taste for it and would enjoy being in that field of work. Now when it comes to circumstances closing in on your choices, you have entrance exams that you have managed to clear, fees that is affordable to your family and availability of all additional funds required for you to be able to study in the university of your choice. Though these seem like circumstance working in your favour, it actually is the complete opposite. These are all things that will eventually prevent the entire idea of observation and exploration. It is all systematically pushing you into a choice that was never your own, that is, to be an engineer. Now, when it comes to conditioning or acquired taste closing in on your choices, it is much more brutal. You have never thought of maybe being an actor or say a doctor or an entrepreneur for that matter. Let us put aside the fact of whether you have the required skills or not, the bitter truth is that you never even thought of being one.

It is understandable that there are plenty of academic and career oriented courses available in the world and you cannot possibly explore all of them but the question remains that did you ever even have a choice? A choice to be able to explore? Sometimes it is tragic that your financial situation does not allow you to make a choice which is circumstance closing in and we feel there isn't much one can do about it. Then there is our conditioning which frames our mindset in such a way that we abstain from that exploration. These are yet again unbreakable bonds that prevent you from being the best version of yourself. Your mind which is the most powerful entity is essentially capable of doing almost anything. However, when you get choices like in terms of the college you would prefer, you feel like life has given you a choice but it is essentially a mere illusion of choice.

When your decisions stop being guided by the magnetic pull of an external entity, when you're willing to shift zones and explore the pull of all the choices you have in that particular circumstance, when a new choice has managed to entangle itself into your periphery and its exploration becomes your choice, is when you're finally free from this 'who you think you are' and now, an entire universe of 'who you can be,' will be available for you. You would in fact then be free to explore what the universe has in store for you instead of being a slave to your constructed self.

It is truly a beautiful feeling when after taking that leap of faith one ends up finding beauty in something one wouldn't normally choose to do, but if you don't find anything of that sort then you can still feel glad about how you managed to dismantle your constructed self of acquired tastes and are now on the quest to finding yourself.

It could be a beautiful feeling to sit in the sun with your mother and it could be fun just going out for lunch with your friend but you need to have the willingness to explore all your choices and find more into what you are all about. There is nothing wrong with being an engineer but, to be an engineer should never be the goal of your life because it was never your choice in the first place. You were systematically placed there by certain forces of the universe. The same universe is constantly opening new doors for you, if you can gain the ability to observe carefully every choice that entangles itself into your environment.

The fact remains that most people enjoy being an engineer and feel proud as well. Most people also enjoy watching their favorite show. The intention is not to discourage any of those choices that you have made but to attain a certain sense of clarity about whether you really made that choice or not. To know anything on those lines you've got to know who you really are before you make any of those choices. The sad truth is that our schools don't educate us in that domain and we end up making most of our choices in life before finding ourselves. Finding yourself should be the true goal of your life before a constructed version of yourself lives your entire life on your behalf. Without an understanding of yourself life can become a pile of regrets as you grow older and wiser. However, it is never too late to begin finding yourself because one can make the best of life whenever one meets their true self. Our self is a puzzle that needs to be crafted very carefully. Whatever we are or become is picked up from the world outside and that world is huge. Everything is an acquired taste in that sense. You see something, like it and make it a part of yourself which again is essentially a choice made. Would it not be unfair if you never get to explore before you choose the first thing you like?

Even when we sit to watch a TV show or a film we browse through the internet till we find something that really clicks with us. Should not life as a whole be given that choice of exploration through this vast universe around us till we really feel sure about what we have chosen? Our constructed self is a combination of things we liked or found necessary to build our selves and it has already made quite a few choices on our behalf. This rewiring of our minds now has become relevant. What becomes imperative at this point is the act of distancing yourself from everything you thought you were and reimagining the puzzle of your 'self' by keeping the best of your pieces and discarding the ones that were pushed onto your personality by circumstance and conditioning. Then as new choices arise, this new you would be open to observe them carefully and explore them completely before letting them enter as a new piece in the puzzle of your self. To create your self may not give you everything you need from life but it will surely tell you much more about what you really want from it.

Most people have no idea about what they want from life. Those who think they do are also mostly under an illusion that they know. Their choices are not their own and their self is a mere construct. When you know what you really want from life and are making your choices with careful observation then you are already more awake than most people. The joy of knowing yourself in itself exceeds all other joys in life. As you calmly traverse through all the choices the universe will offer to you, you would soon find that there is so much more to you than you had expected. Then you may not be the most successful person in monetary terms but on a spiritual plane you would exceed most others. You will choose what you do and who you are as a person altogether. You will know true joy. Then again, like everything else, it is a choice that you make, whether you wish to be in chains of circumstance and conditioning or that you choose who you are and finally be free.

□

## *Chapter 3*
# String Theory and Thoughts

When we talk about will power, the fundamental question is, "Are you in control of your mind or does your mind control you?", but before we even begin to address something like 'will power,' the more pertinent questions are, "are your thoughts even your own?" or "is not most of what we think mere clutter?", "What about thoughts that get initiated without instigation?" and "How much of our thought process can we even control?"

Well, the mind is an extremely powerful processor and no one is completely in control of it and it doesn't even benefit you to be in total control of it. Total control would mean shutting off your DMN and taking control of all the things that your mind can subconsciously do on its own to assist you. Such extreme measures make no sense and that isn't the implication here when we talk about taking control of your mind.

Our minds have been conditioned for years now and taking control simply means a certain rewiring of our brains. Our stream of consciousness is a network of strings that works on the basis of association which may even seem random at times. So what is this 'stream of consciousness'?

In essence, when you are driving that car, while your DMN is handling the driving part of it, your stream of consciousness is the part that is thinking of a song, the song connects to a memory which is associated with the song and the connection may or may not make sense to you and could very well be absolutely random. There is so much data available in your mind which is connected with each other through a vast network of strings or segways within which this stream traverses.

Now, these could all have been temporary files in our mind but through our conditioning, external/ societal pressure and our lack of awareness we have managed to acquire a vast amount of clutter as well. This basically means that our mind is in control of us because our thoughts are running wildly in a cluttered network of strings.

There are people who will tell you that such critical thinking is a privilege and life is to be lived simply, but the truth is that they are the ones who have complicated their lives to such an extent that self awareness to them is not even much of a priority anymore. Everything in this universe is connected, from the first protoplasm to the peak of the evolution of this human mind, it is all just nature evolving to understand and know itself. Our minds are simply mediums through which it can be done.

The philosophy offered here is to help you find oneness with the universe, simplify living and not worry too much, but if you are too attached to the clutter in your mind, luxuries of the world outside and are driven with ambition to get them then none of this will make any sense to you.

So, the question is, "why do we entertain this clutter?"

Well, we don't do it intentionally to say the least. Think of all your thoughts as one dimensional strings. They are connected with each other, vibrate to a certain frequency and interact with each other as well. They can vibrate in unpredictable different ways and there is no set pattern of how one thought is connected to the other. These strings in their vibrational states also embody a gravitational force or a certain pull which is what connects a song to a memory in a flash of a second and in a way that sometimes the song and the memory are so unrelated that the connection cannot be explained.

Apart from association, there is also a sense of inception happening here. Say you're sitting in your room and reading a book and out of the blue you feel like having a chocolate. Psychologists will tell you that your addiction to it is causing chemicals in your brains to rise and are in turn demanding that chocolate. However, all these professionals hardly talk about the inception that just happened and the central concern is so unaddressed and overlooked almost by everyone that it is frankly absurd. You would say, "I need to be stronger and have to develop the will to fight my own mind that is craving for chocolates" but the issue still remains unresolved. The question is, " Why on earth is my mind asking for a chocolate when I am reading a book?" and more importantly, "Why am I entertaining this clutter in my mind?". If you could just ask this question to yourself then that is all the 'will power' you will ever need to reorganize your mind because of the sheer weirdness and stupidity with which these inceptions occur.

The chocolate is not the problem here, the problem is the inception of an idea ungoverned by you and an irrelevant connection made by your brain due to an overflow of clutter inside your mind. Once you have figured out what is happening in your mind then you will almost every time be aware of your own thoughts. In fact, once you gradually rewire your brain, you will have space for your own thoughts and eventually the next time you eat a chocolate, the decision will be your own.

This clutter in your mind has no limits. The chocolate analogy was the simplest way to put through the idea that most of your thoughts are not your real thoughts. This random influx of thoughts can vary from missing your lover to just a melody of a song that gets stuck in your head. Anything that occurs in your mind without your conscious effort is probably clutter. So how do we work on discarding clutter and gaining control of our minds?

Apart from meditation, you have to ensure that you are in control of what you infuse your mind with. If you are busy binging a TV series to relieve stress then the next episode will always be a priority in your mind and it will constantly demand for it. Your favorite series is already a part of all the clutter in your head now. All your habits are potential clutter that demand for the release of 'happy hormones.' You are basically addicted to the 'dopamine' that releases in the process of having fun. It is an addiction similar to the intake of drugs. Be it your morning coffee, going out with friends, watching shows or eating that chocolate. Sitting silently and being with your mind is another way to relax which may seem undoable or less fun than any other activity. However, once you develop the taste for it, gradually it will become a beautiful feeling. If you can release the same dopamine in such a natural manner then your happiness will stop being dependent on external entities. Apart from that your mind will be a calmer place with much less noise. Your brain will be rewired so to say, thought patterns will begin to take shape and concentration levels will be much higher than before.

We've all had those moments when we were talking about something and the chain of thought simply breaks. We lose connection to what we were talking about and recollecting it is just not possible. The strings that connect one thought to another often go through such glitches. So, losing touch of what we consciously want to talk about is natural and most of these glitches will continue to operate in that manner. Which is to say that when you are reading that book, the thought of eating a chocolate will still occur. The only difference is that this time you would be more aware of where that thought came from.

You can only change the food for your mind so to say. You can merely change what you infuse it with. It works on weirdly connected strings, the pattern of which is unpredictable. Thoughts are unpredictable too and every once in a while you will have to struggle with them. In essence, your awareness of the existence of your thoughts and their operating style is the only tool you have in your arsenal to take control of your mind.

What you need is to be able to distinguish between thoughts that are your own and the instincts of your mind. Now you don't need to completely discard all your instincts. You will still go out with your friends, watch your favorite TV series and eat chocolates too. You will most certainly still have days when you want to relax and actually have fun. You have all the right to do that. The difference is that your mind was running on an auto mode where you were a slave to your instincts, but now whether those instincts are to be entertained or not, will be your choice and even though the processor of your mind will remain the same, the one running it would be you.

□

# ON SOCIETY

## *Chapter 4*

# The Dirt Realm and the Struggle for Survival

We may believe that an understanding of our nature, our choices and a control over our mind is easily more than enough to go through life smoothly. However, when we talk about social set-ups and dissolving into them, it is a battlefield which frankly we are still not prepared for. Out in the world, every person has the capacity to instigate you. It takes mere seconds to lose control of who you are. You may easily forget who you are supposed to be. You would discard the wiser choices in situations and lose sanity over the most pettiest things. Conflict is literally waiting for you at every step. Could it possibly be avoided? Why does human interaction have to be so hostile and more importantly why does taking the high road seem so impossible during these conflicts?

Now, we don't always choose who we interact with and our surroundings often put us within the noise around us. The world is filled with people who would like to drag you down into their arenas and seek pleasure out of the approval of their audience.

Most people get a kick out of the appreciation they get from the people around them, to the point that it is what they live for and all their pleasure depends on it. When that happens we forget who we really are and are DMN steps up to be the Defense Mechanism to our Ego. Social survival within this new realm is now a major concern to us and we rush into it to seek acknowledgement from an audience just to fit in. Your responses in such situations start becoming instinctive. You start responding to this noise just so your voice can be heard within it. You crave to be a respected part of this group now and for that you are willing to perform for this audience that was never yours. This crowd is not interested in who you really are and they merely want to see you dance like an idiot within the shape that they have designed for you. Man being a social animal prefers to fit in within its kind. However, it often ends up being a complete abandonment of our individuality and we become a part of the herd.

One would think, "why should I dance to their tunes and why should I step into this dirt at all?". Well, you don't need to but it is easier said than done. Survival within the world while keeping your self intact is not really a cakewalk. There are factors that you need to take into consideration despite knowing who you really are. The dirt realm is a battlefield of social survival. In reality, one often needs to create a DMN or a Social Self in order to survive or even feel happy at the end of a day.

Now, every person has an energy, an aura or a certain frequency at which they vibrate. This might end up sounding like absolute pseudo science but from this moment on you will soon realise how real this is the next time you interact with any person. Interaction in fact, affects you to the point that you can only be the amount of yourself that fits within the restrictions of their aura. You're inside their magnetic field so to say and your energy has now transformed to fit in within the limits of their perception of you. In fact you're so comfortable with it and so involved in that interaction that you often don't realise that your shape has been altered by someone else's aura. To put all this simply, when you think of the phrase 'A man is the company he keeps' in the current context, you will realise how far away you end up drifting from who you are just by indulging into day to day social interaction.

The question then is "how do we keep our selves intact when we encounter such situations?"

Let us say that a group of people constantly pick on you at your workplace. There are certain power dynamics at play and there is a leader of that pack that ensures to take a shot at you every now and then. Now, there are two ways to approach this. Firstly, you must understand that these people are just trying to have some fun. Despite it being at your expense it is still casual fun and entertainment that they are looking for. What you could do here is learn to laugh at yourself and not take yourself too seriously. Eventually you will find yourself in a club, dissolving smoothly into this pack that seemed so intimidating at first.

Secondly, if you do not want to be a part of this group at all then you could choose to ignore their shots and learn to pity them because this is what they live for. They will never think beyond casual fun. You merely have to smile at them once in a while and they will eventually stop when it stops being fun. In time it will stop as long as you never forget to smile at them.

However, this is merely the case of a general interaction. When we think about arguments and differences of opinion, it is a whole new mess of dirt slinging. Think of a person as an atom, the nucleus has protons or the listening abilities of a warm person and neutrons or the warm way of their disagreement, agreement or an alternate point of view. However all of this is surrounded by electrons with a negative charge which is the aggressive assertion of people all around the world who think they know best. You could open up your social media for live examples available in the comments section of absolutely anything really.

So then what could be done when you have a social image to keep intact, when we look for promotions and social mobility from life, when we feel the need to be acknowledged by the people around us or when we are dealing with workplace politics? What happens when taking the high road means being stepped on and facing constant humiliation? Is not the fear of abandonment by the society around us real or do we just form some sort of machiavellian neutrality where we hide our true selves and pretend to be someone else for survival in this realm?

The central issue here is that whether it is pleasing people, getting into an aggressive argument or being a neutral bystander, all these choices are never yours. Your DMN literally does not even need an invitation to roll around in this mud. It would do this to protect its ego or seek pleasure of other people's approval and as pertinent as these questions are, as long as we are looking at our selves through a stranger's lens, we will remain vulnerable and lost.

Let us say that you have gotten into an argument with a person. He is getting aggressive with his stance and is being rude to you as well. Firstly when it comes to an argument it takes two people for it to last. Secondly, you need to understand where that person is coming from and what his stance is all about. This way you will in all probability learn to empathize with him because you understand why he is saying whatever he is saying. Finally, even if you think that maybe he is incorrect about what he is saying, he has still very strongly, already made up his mind about what he believes in and you cannot possibly change his mind with just your words anyway. So, you could only empathise with him for he is oblivious and will not entertain other points of view on the matter.

It is mostly about angling our perception, about how we are looking at these things. The truth is that everyone who has ever been rude to you or tried to put you down is dealing with the same issues of trying to keep their selves intact. A little warmth and empathy has never hurt anyone. When you face a conflicting situation then the best thing you can do is try and understand why someone was getting aggressive with you in the first place. You have to shut off your 'ego defense mechanism' in such cases and pause to think why it happened. When you begin to empathize with your opponent you will realise that you don't have to step into his arena at all. What he offered was an invitation to 'the dirt realm' which you can refuse to accept and be warmer towards him.

More importantly, as long as you're viewing your 'self' based on what other's opinion of you might be, you will constantly be at war with yourself because you're fretting over an assumption and your concerns are assumptions too. You can never please everyone even if you constantly try to fit in for the sake of your audience. If the warmth towards everything and everyone around you comes from within then you can breeze through this aggressive realm effortlessly and when you realise the futility of all the unnecessary conscious efforts you put in to be a people pleasing, approval seeking success in life, then you can find the time and the headspace to begin to think beyond just this realm.

This realm is just a small segment of life but most people make their whole lives about it and therefore never reach the thinker realm. So in a certain sense, it is also imperative that you find people that resonate with your frequency so that your 'self' remains alive and gets the right kind of interaction and in the right amount to grow, or you might end up forgetting who you are altogether and become the shape of either how the world wants to see you or how you want the world to see you.

There is an old saying that if you wish to fight a pig then you will have to step into the dirt. The 'dirt realm' is full of invitations to battles that are best left not entertained. Society will constantly put challenges in your path in the form of conflicts. The question is "are you willing to lose out on how you define yourself for the sake of your ego?"

To get into a conflict is, more often than not, your personal choice. We feel helpless because we feed our ego too much. We want to be seen as a strong, respectable character, out on the world stage. Though that character is a construct created to appear in a certain light to our audience and not our true self. It has been instigated and pulled out from within us. When we start thinking beyond our performance and stop taking our character so seriously is when we can add some fluidity to it. Dissolving smoothly into any social scenario, then occurs naturally and taking the high road, then comes easily to us because that urge to feed our ego disappears. Once we realise that we are not here to perform in order to keep a social image intact, we can truly be our selves and sidestep all conflict with ease.

□

## *Chapter 5*

# The Thinker Realm and the Burden of Knowledge

Firstly, everything that exists within this universe can be wondered about, questioned or looked at critically. Secondly, very few people choose to do that. So if you are a thinker, then to find your kind is not an easy task either. It is also true that being a thinker despite all hurdles in the way is a privilege that not all can enjoy. The opportunity to think about things can only be gained once your survival is taken care of. That being said, it still isn't impossible and you might still find a thinker who is struggling for survival and yet wonders about the nature of our reality and has a lot to say. The reason why you don't find too many people within this realm is because they find it pointless, have a short attention span and the intellectual discourse that people within this realm enjoy so fondly, takes a heavy toll on their minds. They'd rather socialise or enjoy light humour at the expense of each other or a stranger.

So why does a thinker arise? What makes a thinker different from the herd?

A thinker's willingness to learn alone becomes his biggest drawback that draws him away from the crowd. He is a great listener and when among the crowd, he has to constantly filter trash that comes along the way in the name of a conversation. Within the realm a conversation is usually a learning experience and is a product of an underlying mutual respect that one thinker has for another. The pleasure derived from such a conversation is as fulfilling as any other pleasure that you can think of. More importantly, it is what keeps their individuality intact. It helps them remember who they are, how they think and what they talk about. It is a quotient that needs to be satiated as much as say the satiation of emotional quotient of someone who has fallen in love. Their mind often then yearns for an interaction within the realm. They need someone that resonates with their frequency. Such social interactions become an outlet or a release for them.

The irony is that what can be considered stressful for most people, who would come home from work and maybe enjoy some gentle comedy, a beer and a light conversation, is actually what releases the stress of a thinker. He would rather sit alone and watch something cerebral that stimulates his brain. He would enjoy the company of someone similar.

The heaviest burden is the burden of knowledge and when not shared it can destroy your mind and make you lose your individuality as well. When you know something that few people do then you feel this natural urge to share that knowledge and you also feel the need to find that one person who is interested in it. Then, that becomes your outlet for release. it is like you've eaten something heavy and this outlet becomes the digestive process. Only when you've shared what you've learned, can that material be digested in your mind and you can feel the release which finally relaxes you. An intellectual discourse is a fulfilling acquired taste unlike any other and when you get the hang of it, then it is almost impossible to go back to anything else. It can get as aggressive or assertive as an argument at times but the underlying mutual respect beneath that disagreement will eventually align those paths, till a systematic deconstruction reaches a crescendo of a conclusion. The essence, in this case, is a collective thirst for new knowledge or an alternate point of view where the argument is never really an ego battle.

An aggressive thinker can only be respected in this realm and will seem like an egoistic person to everyone in the 'dirt realm.' He will end up pushing away everyone with his demeanor which has less to do with his attitude and more about how much he knows. The truth is that no one is interested in any of that knowledge as it is and the dirt realm is all about ego battles and social image because of which he can never fit in. He calls out things for what they are and ends up being disliked by everyone.

However, that never unsettles him in the least because he knows who he is, he knows the realm that he belongs to and he doesn't mind standing up for his ideologies even though he knows the futility of wasting his energy in the 'dirt realm' and despite the toll it might take on his brain he remains hopeful because at the end of it all, it is the burden of knowledge that he is carrying which needs to be shared and he is helpless in that sense because he can't be anything other than himself.

So how does 'the thinker' survive in the dirt realm?

Firstly, you have to ask yourself, are you a thinker at all? When we talk about thinkers then we are not looking down on everyone else. If you are a cheerful social person and have found your place in society then this section is not for you. If you like to keep things light and find joy without worrying too much then you don't need to change yourself in any way.

Now, if you are a thinker then you need to ask yourself what kind of a thinker are you? Are you an assertive orator? Are you a calm listener? Are you a little bit of both? or Are you more or less a loner?

Most assertive orators and loners can never tolerate stupidity or unnecessary chatter.

They cannot bear to survive in the dirt realm and often avoid it completely. They need people that resonate with their kind of thought flow and people who can hold an intellectual discourse. They are essential pieces of the thinker realm and never choose to leave their domain. To them being stuck in any superficial environment is a nightmare. Moreover, they long for the release of letting go of the burden of knowledge which is unavailable in the dirt realm. The people within the dirt realm also find 'thinkers' obnoxious and complete bores. So in a certain sense, such thinkers desperately need their own realm to survive and grow.

When it comes to calm listeners and fluid thinkers, they are a little more tolerant and even empathetic at times. They accept people for who they are and don't always need to unload the burden of knowledge.

A calm listener is someone who takes in anything that comes his way and filters it accordingly without complaining about his atmosphere. He can easily step outside his domain and even if sometimes he doesn't enjoy the experience completely, he is still more understanding towards the people around him. Intellectual discourse maybe a preference in his case but a light banter or a little stupidity is bearable to him. So when his kind is unavailable to him, he easily dissolves within the kind that is available.

A fluid thinker is not very different from a calm listener in most aspects. However he is more of an alpha male in his approach. He knows what he wants and also knows how to get it. He is in a certain sense the bridge between the two realms. He has the capacity to convert people into thinkers. He enjoys being in his realm but when he is surrounded by other normal folk he will know how to smoothly dissolve into their domain. He is a likable personality as compared to most other thinkers. His warm nature is lauded by people in the dirt realm and every once in a while, if he gets hold of any one of them alone, he can make intellectual discourse a likable experience and he can strike up a conversation that maybe well out of the other person's domain. He is usually well respected in both domains and doesn't have trouble drifting in and out of them. He doesn't naturally hate stupidities and banters. He is someone who has learned to enjoy both aspects of life and understands that different people have different tastes and he is flexible in morphing his persona depending on where he is in a moment. The burden of knowledge, however, is something that even a fluid thinker needs to unload. However he has a way of getting around it and finds a way to make it interesting even for someone in the dirt realm.

Technically, the thinkers don't really need the dirt realm at all and it is important for them to find their own kind so that they can be themselves. The two realms are separate for a reason. Different people have different interests and in a general sense everyone has to find their kind. There is no point in trying to please people who are not your audience and punishing yourself with a social circle that isn't meant for you. Warmth and empathy, on the other hand, are helpful tools to let you understand newer perspectives and help you see people in a new light. With an open mind one can be socially fluid and would be comfortable interacting with almost anyone. At the same time too much interaction with people who are not your kind will, in all probability, have an impact on your personality and you will stop being who you are if your social needs are not satiated. A thinker is a thinker after all and he will most definitely need someone similar to resonate with. He will need an outlet to unload the burden of knowledge. This may sound improbable, but the burden is like food that needs digestion in the form of interaction and undigested knowledge can make you go insane.

So essentially, all thinkers suffer from this burden and hence are a little different from the crowd. Loners especially more so because they function on a level beyond interaction, which is quite close to insanity, which is why most people find them weird. However, they end up being extremely interesting people when you do end up talking to them. Within the realm loners are the most respected, they are extremely selective about who they interact with and they have mastered the skill of digesting knowledge without an outlet. They speak when spoken to and only say something that really needs to be said. They are respected within the realm because they don't need the dirt realm at all and at the same time they can function without the thinker realm as well. They never have a problem surviving in any realm as they are self aware and satisfied with who they are. They can easily be confused with loners within the dirt realm who are longing for a connection and simply lack confidence. A loner in the thinker realm is a loner by choice and self sufficient in every way.

Survival, as you may have noticed, is not something that bothers thinkers. They are tactful in keeping their selves intact while surviving. They find outlets for relieving the burden of knowledge or in some cases learn to carry it. This burden is their curse that makes them often unbearable to most but at the same time it is also what defines them as people. Hence, there is this certain layer of social conflict in between the two realms. The conflict which arises from the fact that both realms are extremely judgmental of each other and find the other one superficial. Survival then becomes a choice, that you either choose your realm, avoid them all completely or be fluid enough to float through it all with ease. What is required then is to realise and ask yourself, who you really are as a person and where do you see yourself in all this? Once you know who you are, you would be quite comfortable with where you are despite the inherent, unresolvable conflict between the two realms.

□

## *Chapter 6*
# Failure and the Bottom

What is failure? How do you really define the term? Is it calculated based on initial schooling and academics? Is it based on acquiring a job? Is not the term absolutely vague if we don't take into account any generic norms that define it?

The pleasure you derive from being successful at anything is enough to help you get by. It becomes, ultimately, the joy that everyone seeks. We chase after it by pushing ourselves. Now, you could say that all the questions about life, existence and self only come to unsuccessful people because they have lost the race and the chance to feel that joy of success. This might just be true, but the mind that can push itself and get that joy of achieving what they aimed for is obviously capable of so much more. In a sense, all people who are successful at anything, have limited their options of all that they could be. Their idea of pleasure and purpose is limited to their respective domain.

Say, a person is a successful software developer. He was always doing good academically and now he chose an area of expertise and is doing well at his job. His role in society has now been fixed. He will always be just that. He does not have the scope to entertain the thought that maybe he could have been something else and in a sense, he never gets the space to search for his self or what it really wants. These are the people who have their path laid out for them and they give it their best to reach the finish line. Once they have made it, how long could the pleasure of achieving a job at say a big software company really last? They were young and naive when they made their choice of path and now one can't help but think that this man, who is so good at what he does, would have probably been equally good at something else, but now he cannot worry himself with the road not taken. The truth is that this man lacked the courage to carve out his own path because the risk of failure was much higher in those terrains. He wanted to be practical and most importantly he needed a map with every step of the way well drawn out, a constant state of guidance, assistance and a sense of security so to say. Now you see him looking for sweet escapes by traveling, soul searching and all those little things that he missed out on because his pleasure of achieving, that very thing, that he worked so hard for is not enough anymore.

The truth is that whatever well drawn out path that is offered to us by the society comes with an extreme amount of societal pressure. Since we live among them, their approval gradually, out of pressure becomes a necessity for us. Even a day's worth of happiness starts requiring this approval. In this illusion, we are made to believe that this approval means something. We start thinking that this pressure, that is being exerted upon us, is probably backed by the fact that these people are concerned about us. If you look at it carefully though, this pressure is only ruining lives by making sure that no one lives up to their potential. It is spawning a generation of sad souls who are unsure of what they are looking for and another of oblivious people who are satisfied with the approval of their peers and the society around them. In that sense, failure is quite subjective as a concept. The question then is 'who has failed really?'. Did we not collectively fail as a society?

Now, let's say you've failed in your initial years. You're immediately looked down upon by your peers. You're considered foolish by everyone and in a very natural way, you're also made to believe that you are one. You lose all your self confidence. In such a state, there is hardly any possibility for you to be able to perform well even if you could. The impact of failure at any age is pretty similar. It is these very people whose concern begins to destroy your ability to believe in yourself or even see things clearly. These people have set standards of success in well laid out paths and the fact that you sway from them is unacceptable and is, essentially, what is considered failure. Nobody knows what you're meant to be and exploring that domain isn't an option either. In essence, all your schooling is merely people telling you ways to fit into society's economic and social systems. If you're not interested in any of them, then you are labeled a distracted student. The truth is that society is often a failure in understanding you and your needs.

Regardless, being a failure really gives a positive turn to your life. With your abandonment also comes your experience of touching rock bottom. Say, you ran the rat race and didn't fit into any of the paths laid out and you also failed to acquire a decent job, then you've reached quite a privileged position in life. Firstly, at the bottom, things cannot get any worse. So no matter how hard it seems, you will eventually come to terms with reality and accept your fate. Secondly, once you've done that you have the option to carve out your own path from scratch which is an opportunity that most 'successful' people don't have and some even long for. Carving out your own path has its risks and is not an easy task, but if you choose to do so, then you have nothing to lose because you're already at the bottom. Some might say that this is only valid for people whose economic needs are taken care of but such an idea stems from a mind that has always prioritised economic needs. Someone who has actually seen rock bottom is least concerned about his financials and once he has accepted his reality then he becomes flexible enough to accept any profession with humility. He has the time to observe and see things clearly. He gains a new perspective on life and self. His experience becomes his wisdom and his willingness to accept anything that comes his way is, what becomes his core strength.

Now, we've established that failure is a privilege, but in what sense? How does failure really benefit anyone? Well, we shall get to that gradually, but before we begin to understand failure, we must first understand success.

So, what is success?

We have discussed a couple of analogies and they surely suggest that in a general sense success is fitting in to the social and economic system of the society we live in. You are successful, if you are capable of fulfilling your financial needs, through a medium of profession, that is acceptable and respectable in the eyes of the society you live in. You are successful, furthermore, if you manage to get married into a decent household. In general terms, that is all that there is to the idea of success. It is majorly weighed in monetary terms. The more money you have, the more successful you are considered.

Success actually is quite a broad term if you think about it. Say, to have a successful and loving relationship, it takes more than just getting married into a decent household. To have a successful career, it depends on the amount of joy your job gives you. To know what you want from life, it takes a successful exploration before you even begin to understand happiness in its essence and to have a wholesome and successful life, surely, it takes more than the amount of money you have.

To be recognised as successful and to actually be successful are two completely different things. To actually have a sense of the way of the world, one needs to touch rock bottom and in fact succeed at failing. To know that despite all its efforts, you didn't fit into the social and economic system is a success in its own right. It means, you have literally stepped out of the system now. You can now begin to explore all your options within this vast universe. You can begin to discover what you were looking for in life and where you really want to be. When you are carving out your own path towards your own definition of success, you will know that it, surely, has to be beyond money and a married life.

Could success really be defined by a social set-up of a rat race?

Once you've finished the race, you find the daily existence in this setup tedious, monotonous and joyless. What is the point of racing for something that is not even fulfilling and could you even call it success after that? Would you not rather fall in the middle of the race to find out that the race is pointless? Your failure in this race is the greatest gift life could have given you because you get the time to pause and think about where you were going and where you could be. Once you begin to wonder about the latter, a whole new universe opens up for you and then your happiness becomes more valuable than the world's expectations from you. The pressure of society will always be there and you will most certainly have days when you face self doubt. However, you need to remember that you are not a part of that race and this pressure is exactly how society pulls you into the trap of being a 'cog in the wheel' and having no individual identity.

To strive for carving your own path, is the road not taken in most people's lives and since you are surrounded by them, their criticism of your choices is something that you can never escape. However, as long as you know what you're looking for and are willing to strive for it, you can ignore all the noise along the way. Happiness can be found in the humblest of professions and money beyond a point is unnecessary. The joy you are really looking for, can be found within you, once you begin to see your life through your own lens and not the one, the world around you uses to see your life and choices. They cannot be expected to understand your choices, simply because they did not have the courage to make those choices themselves. After you have reached the rock bottom, your path though long, hard and filled with criticism, will be unique and different because you would have carved it yourself. Along that way, you will find yourself meeting that happiness which most successful people yearn for and the walk would, then, seem worthwhile.

□

## *Chapter 7*

# The Realm of Torture and the Illusion of Reality

Apart from the dirt realm and the thinker realm there is another realm that is specifically reserved for people that have been through failure. Failure that is not just a minor setback but rather one that has given them enough time to pause and self reflect. Self reflection to the point that they stop believing in themselves. A point where they begin to doubt themselves and their capabilities.

Self reflection after failure can be quite an impactful experience. It can take you to the depths of your rock bottom. Every once in a while, a man who has failed and has had the time to think about it, reaches these depths. It can trigger depression because he has shut his DMN off, which basically means that he has let his guards down and let the world get to him. He is so vulnerable and humble at this point that he would literally believe absolutely anything, as his self worth has been misplaced. He would think that he was probably too arrogant to see things clearly, that life has showed him his place and he would consider this as some kind of reality check.

Seeing other people's success and drawing unreasonable comparisons can lead him to believe that he is the most foolish person on the planet and within such conclusions, his confidence is lost too. More often than not this happens to people who have a very grand self image. They are the ones who believed in themselves and the fact that they really are exceptionally talented. The realm of torture is one where a man is alone in a torture device for his mind which he creates himself.

The truth is that such people very often are really talented and their circumstances have pushed them into these dark corners of self doubt and sadly not all of them make out of it. What one thinks of himself is heavily dependent on his circumstances. However, in all this vulnerability, the easiest drift from truth is to believe that maybe you aren't exceptionally talented, maybe you are the most foolish person and surely you were an oblivious man who has come to his senses with an epiphany.

With success comes the belief that you are something and with a catastrophic failure comes the loss of self worth. So in that sense, it is your place in the society that defines your perception of reality. So in a certain sense, your failure isn't even relevant as it is a circumstantial movement to a tougher period in your life, if you look at this objectively. You have been now placed in a position where you are bound to consider yourself a fool because in terms of circumstance, you are getting nothing that is required to be successful at all. Even the smartest man, put in your position would end up nowhere because we all need circumstantial crutches to get anywhere in life. With all the great struggle stories you've heard, you will find one thing common in all of them that without a little help from someone no one has made it anywhere in the world. You've just been left limping in this world while your crutches have been snatched, which means that your failure is most certainly not your fault.

Your perception of your failure is what has created the realm of torture for you because you are oblivious to the nature of things and more importantly, you are not viewing your reality from a distance. Reality is an emotionally powerful experience. It sucks you in along with your perception and leaves you blinded to the truth. The only way to escape the illusion of reality is to keep your objective distance while viewing it. That is to say that you don't live your reality all the time but instead step outside and view it from an outsider's perspective. Not just any random generic outsider's perspective, which might just agree that you are a failure, but rather a critical one, where you see that these outside forces of circumstance need to be in your favour before you make it to where you're meant to be in life.

In these tougher periods of life, everyday could be a war when you're battling with self doubt. However, when you accept your reality humbly without losing the truth of who you are, half the battle is won. When you realise that you could be successful wherever you land in life and you could be a failure even at the top of the world, in time you will see that where you are in life and where you're meant to be are not very different places and they are both equally beautiful if you choose to believe so. To put it simply, how you look at your life and the circumstances around it, pretty much, define what your life is. Everything else is just emotional confusion, created by the pressure of the outside world that wants to see you in a particular light. Moreover, you have been conditioned to live up to their standard definition of what success is, which is a limited perception of reality.

Reality is a vast expanse where success and failure are mere constructs. They don't even mean anything if we view reality from such a vantage point. Viewing your life from such a distance may make you realise the insignificance of your life as a human but it also helps you break the chains of conditioning and societal pressure, for it helps you find success in the life you have, before you begin to reach for the life you wish to have.

So, then what exactly happens in the realm of torture and what is this illusion of reality?

The bright side to the realm of torture is that if you make it out of it then you begin to have a much clearer perspective on life. It is a place where you enter believing that you are the smartest man alive on the planet and there is nothing beyond you. Your confidence and self belief is on cloud nine. At the same time, during your journey through this realm you face ego loss and begin to think of yourself as the biggest fool as and when you end up facing failure despite your talents. These are both different sides of the dual nature of your self. The experience of failure out in the world makes you believe that you are a fool and the joy of understanding yourself gives you an ego boost and makes you think of yourself as better and higher than everyone else on a spiritual level. There are days where you think of yourself as nothing at all and days where you have the spirit of conquering the world.

Both these extremes are mere illusions of reality since reality is whatever you perceive it to be. Gradually, you begin to understand the dual nature of reality. Finally, you reach a point where you realise that you are extremely foolish and extremely talented at the same time depending on where you circumstances have placed you in reality.

This constant struggle of trying to find yourself is the entire process of self reflection.

Very few people reach this point where they see the duality of their own self. It can only be done if you have failed enough in life to reach a point where you don't really know what you are capable of anymore. The realm of torture is a personalised experience and is very different from the other two realms. The reason why very few make it to this realm is because of the systematic coincidences and variables required to reach this point are too many. Firstly, you need to be someone who is extremely talented and filled with confidence and then you need to fail despite your talents. Then you also have to touch rock bottom. This dual nature then needs to be experienced in isolation. You lose out on friends and there is no source of inspiration in your life either. To put it simply, for you to reach the realm of torture, it is a combination of extreme talent and complete and abject failure in every regard.

The fluidity and flexibility of someone who has been through this realm is unparalleled. He can literally fit in with all kinds of people in society, do all kinds of jobs happily and have a more mature understanding of life than anyone else. He can see reality objectively and he never gets caught up in its illusion. People's opinion and criticism of him do not phase him. He understands both thinkers and people that entertain themselves with little joys of life. He can understand the difference between them and yet fit in with all kinds of people. He could even be completely alone if he has to. He is unafraid to fail at things and he is not worried about his profession, money or even the approval of the people around him. He is completely awake to the experience of the universe. The illusion for him has shattered and he faces every moment with a mature calmness and great humility. The pain of surviving in the realm of torture is immense and filled with self doubt but if you do survive it, then it comes with a sweet release of enlightenment.

Enlightenment teaches you to take things at face value. All your worries regarding success, failure, survival and acknowledgement begin to disappear. Life becomes simpler and your smile never fades. Now, when you are in such a calm headspace even ambition stops being something to be worried about. You smoothly take decisive steps towards it and at the same time, you become indifferent to its achievement. You constantly live in the present moment and the joy it brings. You're always learning and marveling at the nature of the universe around you. This happiness, then, gradually, becomes eternal.

To be in the realm of torture is a tough experience, however if you have the patience to endure it, you will in time, realise that your journey was meaningful. It takes you through all the dimensions of self reflection and tests your metal but by the end of it, it leaves you with an enlightenment that breaks all illusions and paves way to a wholesome personality with strength of character. Your consciousness literally opens doors to a never felt before happiness.

It is said that the best of swords have gone through the toughest of fires and once you have gone through the fires of this realm you realise that you've only come out stronger.

□

# ON BEING

## *Chapter 8*
# Boredom

The human brain is an entity that is active throughout our lives. In a sense it needs to constantly feed on something, be it our own thoughts or immersing into something else. What is boredom then? Is it not the act of us, not providing our mind, with what it is asking of us? Does it not mean that we are in control of our minds in that moment?

In life, we are busy chasing the carrot with a stick at our backs. We want all the joy we can grab before we leave for work the next morning. We are not only tensed and looking for a cure when we get home but the truth is that we also have very short attention spans and we feel the constant need to flood our minds with a distraction. We pace from one distraction to the next, never really embracing the present moment. We discard such ideas by calling them deep or heavy. We miss out on feeling the air around us and the music of the nature that surrounds us simply because it does not suffice our urge for that quick dose of temporary joy supplied by that black screen. We fear being bored.

We keep our minds distracted from reality. To realise the full potential of our minds it is imperative that we come to terms with blankness and silence. The urge to constantly do something comes from the fear of this blankness which we perceive as boredom. In this age, entertainment is at our fingertips. Our definition of relaxing is cluttering our minds with games, movies and anything that appears while we scroll down on social media. It is hard to get bored in this time. We have convinced ourselves that unless we feed our brains with some light, unnecessary randomness, it won't find the relaxation it needs after hours of work.

The truth is that you don't always have to sit seaside or go up the hills to feel nature and its silent beauty. It is as much inside you as you see it outside. Your oneness with nature is just a step away. Before you begin though, you have to overcome that urge of staring at a black screen for content. You have to accept that whatever you're watching is just numbing your mind. You need to begin thinking beyond superficial entertainment. You've got to let all your worries in and face them instead of trying to distract yourself from them. The next time when your brain asks for a quick fix, you've got to step outside your self and take away the carrot that it is longing for. What you have now is your creative space where doing anything is possible. Doing nothing is the most beautiful of things that you could do out here. The life up until this point was based on incentives. Your definition of joy was limited. Boredom can be beautiful if you want it to be.

The intention here is not to discard all joy or never watch a movie or quit social media altogether. The intention is to take command of your mind, to be a more stable person who is not always rushing for that next hit.

Once you've made it to this free space, there will be more time for self reflection, self love and love for everyone around you as well. This is where your journey towards oneness with the universe begins but first you've got to give boredom a chance and embrace it.

So, what is it to be bored?

While some people look for things that can keep them interested and distracted from the silence, there are others that feel bored regardless of the activity around them. Say, there is a party that you are at. Some people enjoy that party and keep themselves from being bored, there are others that can be bored at the party itself. Some people are bored even by a conversation. Some people desperately need their screens to keep themselves going without being bored. This is to say, the shorter your attention span, the more easily you are bored. Boredom is lack of pleasure. We as humans constantly seek pleasure.

We need people to go out with, something to watch, something to eat, something to smoke and our life revolves around these little pleasures. We are so involved in the pleasure of it all, that our mind never has time for the more pertinent questions. We never think about anything like say, our own mortality. The fact that the people we love soon won't be around or that we ourselves are not eternal, are the kind of thoughts that we fear because we don't want to be sad all the time and that is understandable too. However, such thoughts are exactly what can make us cherish the time spent together with our loved ones. To miss them when they are not around or to love them more completely when they are, we need to come to terms with the more real questions.

When you begin to entertain these questions, your conversations with people would gradually become much more real. You would be able to connect with people on a deeper level. The next time you are getting bored at a party you would know that it is an opportunity to have the best conversation of your life with a new person. You would learn to take interest in other people's lives, in the true sense. You wouldn't be just a shallow person making small talk. Your empathy and interest would be more evident and you would also make a new friend.

We as humans most of the times behave like ants. We bump into each other, communicate and then move on to the next person without having any meaningful interaction, because we feel like strangers. Even if there is a meaningful interaction at times, the development of that interaction into a meaningful connection is the last thing on our minds. Every stranger is a potential loved one if you are willing to make that effort. The world is filled with shallow extroverts that wouldn't connect with you beyond that party and complete introverts that couldn't care less about a decent conversation with anyone. In that sense most of us are living like ants. The human mind has developed over centuries of evolution to be able to connect and rediscover communication. If we cannot do that then we are, most certainly, ants at best.

The fact is, you don't have to rush for the next distraction every time you find life getting boring. There is so much more to life than just some happening party. Even a party can be more than just a distraction. The memories of a happening party could also be equally joyous, the memories that you build through real communication at that party. You need to begin to feel more and you also need to think less about the next escape from reality. You would be able to redefine yourself and become a more wholesome version of your self. You could think about say, who you are and feel joyous about your own reflection once you have learned to connect and communicate in the true sense.

When you have learned to be bored is when you could be more open to real interactions. The best of conversations spring up when both people have crossed the barrier of boredom. When two people can appreciate each other's presence and not feel bored is when real communication begins. It is when you understand each other completely and feel connected even within that silence. Such communication only comes to those who are content with their personality and can sit alone and not be bored. It is when you stop finding silences awkward.

The ability to sit with your self is what embracing boredom is all about. The silence completes you. To be able to think about who you are and sit with your thoughts about your self and everything around you, is the kind of reflection that comes when you begin to like yourself. Boredom when embraced can be an enlightening experience. Boredom helps you communicate with your self. It will tell you more about who you are as a person and you will soon begin to move towards the soundness of your own mind as you gradually stop rushing for entertainment and pleasure. You would, eventually, drift away from all distractions and you would begin to enjoy the serenity that your mind has brought you to.

□

## *Chapter 9*
# Pleasure

Our definition of pleasure defines the kind of person we will be in this cosmic existence. We are constantly chasing after pleasure as humans. We feel the need to go out with friends, spend passionate hours with our lover, watch something we enjoy, eat our favourite foods, smoke a cigarette or play games to feel that dopamine release. The truth is that none of this comes with a permanent sense of happiness.

We constantly try to chase for the next hit like an addict but it never lasts. Our habits and interests in turn end up defining us. We never have the time to wonder who we are because we are busy chasing after things in the outside world and looking on the inside never occurs to us. All our interests are in the world outside and that world is huge. In that sense we can never really be done with exploring all that the world has to offer. There will always be something more to buy, some new place to go out with friends and something new to watch on our screens, a new game to play and another cigarette to smoke.

The world outside is so huge that you can always

develop newer interests and then get caught up in them. It is available at your fingertips. You want to watch a stand up show, you want to watch a film, you want to go karting, you want adventure sports, you want to travel and the list goes on and on. Your drive to seek pleasure is never fulfilled. You are never satisfied with what you have. You are looking for the next hit before you have completely enjoyed the last one. So what is it that we're all seeking here and when does it end?

Our reflection is constantly trying to define us but we are so caught up within the material world all around us that we hardly pay attention to it. It is an ignored version of ourselves that is hidden deep within our minds which can also be called the unconscious. It uses twisted ways trying to reach us and get through to us somehow. We are busy surrounding ourselves with people and things that give us joy that the most important part of our personality remains untouched. Our reflection is our completion. We ignore the final piece of our personality's completion and try to fill the void within ourselves with other people and our interests.

If we remain caught up in our interests it will give us pleasure and joy but only temporarily and we will be caught in an endless loop of trying to search for newer interests and people to feel complete. When one TV show ends we are looking for another one. When one playlist is over we look for new songs. We play games that are endless and consuming all our time like everything else. When this doesn't suffice we start meeting people to feel connected. We meet new people for something newer and fresh. All of these are ways to try filling the void inside us that we don't fully understand.

However, like the world outside there is an entire universe inside of us as well. Its fullness is unparalleled and it can give us so much more than what we usually choose, to fill up our voids with. It is reaching out to us but we are deaf to its call because the moment we feel bored, we look for a temporary fix and the world outside has plenty to offer in that regard and the next thing you know, you find yourself chasing after empty pleasures. The call always therefore remains unheard.

Do we ever consider speaking to the mirror, our reflection? Do we consider the possibility that maybe it has something to teach us? Is not another completely different person waiting on the other side to meet us? Where does our confidence lie? Where is our ability to conquer the world hiding? Is it not already waiting on the other side of the mirror?

Well, we have been talking about a certain sense of oneness with the universe but before that we need to consider the dormant universe that lies within us. There is no loneliness in reality because something inside of us is always with us. We only feel lonely because we haven't realised it yet. Our reflection was always capable of filling that void but it never gets its chance and that is because we lack the patience to realise it. We never acknowledge its presence because we never feel it.

Cherishing silence is where this journey begins. Silence paves the path to patience. Whatever you might feel like doing in a moment needs to be shut out and you need to take a pause and sit silently. There is a joy in patience because it leads to the moment when you meet your own reflection. There is a joy in inaction because that is when you're actually spending time with your abandoned self. It is the joy of complete self realization and there is no greater joy once you begin to feel it truly. Its beauty lies in its permanence.

The suggested path sounds undoable and to be honest also like a hoax to the skeptic mind. There will be times when you don't feel anything at all and it will seem boring and a complete waste of time as well. Without that feeling you cannot know it and without knowing it you can't feel it. Your brain at this point is so cluttered with things, people and ideas of the outside world that it needs a complete cleansing. You need to empty your mind completely before your reflection can begin to enter it. To feel any sense of togetherness with your reflection you must first accept that it is a separate entity. You need to acknowledge its presence. It has been ignored for so long that bringing it alive will never be an easy task and before you discard this notion completely just ask yourself if you've ever spoken to the mirror because it has all the answers that you're looking for in this life.

Knowing your 'self' completely is a transcendental experience. To know who you are and what you're capable of is a permanent sense of joy that surpasses all other pleasures. Your pleasure now is one of self love. It is of self confidence. You have now fallen in love with your personality and you can never get enough of it. You are now never bored or lonely but rather always full with the presence of your reflection. You have faith in its abilities. Most of all, you now know that whatever path you're on, there is someone walking right beside you and that you're never alone no matter how tough the road gets. The joy of having the perfect companion who will always be around is a feeling that never fades. It is what true pleasure feels like. It is a confident version of you that is not dependent on external entities for joy. You need to smile at it, make friends with it and harness its power. Your reflection knows you, feels you and understands you like no other. The way to conquer the world outside is to walk hand in hand with the one inside.

Pleasure is essentially just a state of mind. A few chemicals releasing in your brain that are simply giving you the feeling that you are feeling good. That state of mind gets addictive and it becomes something that we are always chasing. The stability to such a state of mind comes when we begin to see worldly pleasures for what they really are. They are mere stimulants that help release certain chemicals in your brain. You move beyond these pleasures as and when you develop the understanding of them. Your mind gradually stops feeling those urges and in time you meet your true reflection. Even your conversations with people grow deeper and more meaningful. Slowly and steadily you begin to understand what true pleasure is. Eventually, you stop chasing after pleasure and let pleasure come to you instead. You then grow enough to feel pleasure even in silence and nothingness.

The implication here isn't that you give up all worldly pleasures and sit in silence forever. The idea is to attain a sense of stability in mind through a sense of 'reflection'. So, the pleasure of say, being at a party, now does not have to be something you chase after. Which means that you only stop feeling the urge, to be at that party, but at the same time, you don't give up going to the party. You let the party happen to you rather than chasing after it. In this way, you essentially, begin to let the universe, bring pleasure to you. The path to this wholesome version of you begins when you stop looking on the outside and begin to look in. Pleasure, then really would be just a state of mind and the ability to feel it eternally, without stimulants, would be yours.

□

## Chapter 10
# Fear

There is no denying that the human brain is the most powerful processing unit in the world. In fact it is the pinnacle of evolution in this universe. Then what is it that holds us back from realising its full potential? Is it our habits? Is it our conditioning? Is it the fact that we don't provide it the right environment to flourish? Is it the world outside that tries to limit our possibilities or is it our own underestimation of this beautiful entity?

We all have this powerful processor at our disposal. The difference then between one person and the other lies in what we feed into it. When we begin to feed fear into it, it is usually a calculated move. We weigh our options, accept our shortcomings and make a fair calculation of our possibilities in life based on our experiences. We have maintained that it is also our circumstances that play a major role in defining our place in the world. Without the circumstances being in our favor and a little help from the world outside we could be the smartest in the universe and still remain completely unknown to the world. This practical and wise calculation in itself is guided by fear. The fear of not making it in the world which in turn distances us from our reflection.

We fear connecting with our true selves because it seems overambitious to us. We are literally using our own minds to set restrictions for its possibilities. We are basically unable to consider the possibility that our mind is limitless and more powerful than any outside force. The mind that is capable of making such a calculated move to find its place in the world and sail smoothly should certainly be able to do much more than that. As ambitious as this endeavour may seem, not pursuing it is an underestimation of the power of the human mind. Your wildest of dreams are only limited by your own fear of complete self realization. There is no pursuit that this clever mechanism is not capable of achieving and this is only the tip of the iceberg. When you begin to develop faith in your reflection, you will begin to see that all your joys are already within you. How you view your brain is eventually what it all depends on.

However, this inward interaction with our reflection scares us because we fear that we will end up being lonely, bored or probably go insane. We desperately cling on to social interactions to keep our sanity intact. It is this constant fear of losing out on people, missing out on life, missing out on what the major segment of the society is into, that limits our potential. The phobia of regretting our decision to be with ourselves for too long haunts us, even though our dreams are just a step away from being fulfilled if we let our reflection in.

When we let go off these fears and finally do have faith in the man in the mirror, then we step into a realm much higher than ambition and begin to feel the beauty of his immaculate presence and the true power of this entity that is our mind. The awareness of our reflection's presence itself comes with such fulfilling clarity that it becomes everything that you need from life. When you begin to see beyond ambition is when everything starts seeming achievable.

So, what is this fear?

As children we are all told to aim big. As life goes on we become wiser and more practical. Our mind is good at calculating and it calculates all the risks of trying to make it big. It calculates all the hassles in the way and begins to understand how this social and economic system works. With a development of this understanding we come to terms with this practical aspect of life that not everyone can make it big. In order to ensure survival we eventually realise that we will have to give in to the way of the system. The major chunk of society works as a cog in the wheel and settles for whatever reasonable profession life offers them. We then have to end up giving up on our dreams to earn a reasonable income and we are willing to settle for something respectable.

Any dream that you have comes with the fear of not being able to achieve it. That fear includes all the hassles that you have to go through along with all the risks that make that dream a long shot. To be a dreamer it requires that you have a willingness to fail. You need to conquer the fear of not being anything at all. Your worries about not having a job or not earning enough are all fears that have no place in the dreamer's mind. It isn't easy being a dreamer at any level. The dreamer has a vision in his mind. A vision needs clarity of mind. To believe in his vision is the most predominant prerequisite.

When you are a dreamer the central concern is that you are all alone with your vision and your belief in your vision. Almost everyone in the world outside are people who have settled for less and will tell you that it is the wise thing to do. With so much noise around your vision, you are bound to have second thoughts about your dream. If you choose to ignore these voices then you would be labelled delusional.

The people in the world outside essentially create this fear in your mind. When they tell you that what you are pursuing is risky. Their experience and wisdom creates a fear in your mind and you begin to consider the possibility that maybe you really are delusional. You doubt your own abilities and begin to underestimate your own mind. As a dreamer you need to have certainty of the fact that as long as you have a vision and you can see it translate into reality, you are most certainly not delusional.

Certainly, there are days when you are battling self doubt but it does not negate the concreteness of your vision. You need to understand that since you are alone, it is a battle between your mind and the world outside. You are literally using your brain to its full potential. The mind has the capacity to win this battle simply because there is nothing more powerful in the world. You simply need to move beyond the fears that exist in the name of pragmatism and wisdom. To do that you need to come to terms with failure. Your dream can only be achievable when you begin to stop fearing failure. Even if you do not achieve your dream, you are still a dreamer. As long as you step into the idea of your vision with a clarity towards failure, doubt and fear will have no place in your mind.

A willingness to fail is what makes a fearless dreamer. His journey begins with an unwillingness to settle for anything less than his dream. The road is tough and he might end up being nothing at all but his joy of knowing what he really is, remains. In the midst of all the battles with self doubt, he learns to understand his own reflection which may seem delusional to the world outside, but it makes him complete. He believes in the power of his mind and its ability to conquer the world and steps into a head on battle with the whole world outside. When he realises that he is this fearless individual, then where he ends up in the world becomes irrelevant, because he is now already content with the reflection of himself. As long as this attitude remains alive, he can also give his all to his vision and the chances of it translating into reality become stronger.

Once you become fearless, you move beyond ambition and your hopes from life. You become satisfied with who you are and have the strength to face the world. Your attitude is what then draws the attention of people around you and you become an inspiration to them. A fearless dreamer is not only capable of fulfilling his dream but also emits an aura of a successful life, no matter what juncture of life he is at.

To be successful at life, you need to have faith in the ability of your mind and contentment with your reflection. Where you land in terms of income and profession then, will have no space in your mind and will be the least of your concerns. There is wisdom that makes you cautious, there is practicality that makes you realistic and then there is fearlessness that makes you complete.

□

## Chapter 11
# Purpose

The beginning of the evolution of the human mind starts from the question 'why?' When we begin to question everything, we begin to distance our selves from the material world and step into the domain of what reality is about. When there was absolutely nothing, there was a sound. It is what we call 'the big bang.' That great sound is the origin of all our beginnings. We are all part of that lasting sound. Sound is the basis of all creation. In a way if we really think about it, we are all mere vibrations. Everything that we see around us is also a mere vibration. That answers how we came to be. However, the question is why we came to be?

It is a natural human instinct to believe that there must be a reason for everything. While science is busy answering the 'whats' of the universe, religion is attempting to answer the 'whys.' Religion is actually built on that attempt and that is why we have so many religious people in the world because we desperately need a reason or a purpose behind things. It scares us to assume that everything is randomly occurring and happens without purpose. Moreover, such a grand design of the universe where life managed to occur with such fine precision makes us wonder that it couldn't possibly be random. The evolution from the first protoplasm to the human mind sure does not seem random. A desire to survive has finally pushed the limits of evolution to the point that we can, as humans, now think and talk about it.

So then, what is our purpose? Why are we here? We are certainly not here for a 9 to 5 job. That is not to say that one shouldn't have a job. However, could it really be all that we are here for?

Purpose is a very fascinating concept that most art forms like films, novels and plays like to toy with. We as a consumer are easily moved by the grand execution of the idea of purpose. Patriotism especially is served to us in such a grand way that every soldier believes that they have a purpose and a destiny to fulfill. To die for one's country is considered an extremely honourable and purposeful act. When you think about it, the whole idea of a conflict between countries seems meaningless. However it is something that is a concrete part of our reality and it won't go away any soon. Either way the idea of purpose is quite interesting when you look at the larger picture and witness artists romanticising it. It is always sold in a way that you end up believing that it means something.

Purpose is considered as a duty or an obligation in most scenarios. Let us say, a woman is a homemaker. Now, it is how she defines herself. Her household obligations become her purpose in life. Let us even take a man, for that matter, say, he works in a big company and he provides for his family. Making sure that his family is financially taken care of is now his prime objective. It has become his purpose in life. To think beyond it is pretty much beyond their capacities. The world around them encourages their efforts and they feel that they are doing the right thing. They assume that maybe this is what life is all about and they happily remain stuck in the system fulfilling their obligations.

We are all caught up in a system that assigns duties to us and we end up assuming that it is our purpose in this universe. Despite the ability of the human mind we end up becoming slaves to this system. We use our minds to fulfill daily duties and never look beyond them. To question our actions does not even occur to us. We are essentially looking for stability in life. We all merely need to be financially taken care of. We struggle to take up jobs that will offer us stability and in time, some social mobility. We keep chasing money till the end of our lives and assume that somehow we are fulfilling our purpose in this universe.

The universe is a vast expanse and in the larger scheme of things, none of what we do matters, if you think about it. We are all aping each others existence and collectively caught up in an assumption that maybe, as a society, we are moving in the right direction. The truth is that independent thought is constantly discouraged and we are expected to fit in the system like sheep, where we all keep moving aimlessly without any real purpose.

From a cosmic point of view, who is to say if

any of us, as existing humans, even had a purpose to begin with? There is no real meaning if we look at it that way. Everything that we know, feel or believe is picked up from the universe around us and we attribute meaning to things. We like to create ideas and notions of being and even spirituality for that matter is merely a constructed concept of being. We created the entire idea of purpose and we do all this to give existence a reason.

Now, with that being said, all philosophy is also put to question as to whether there was any real meaning behind our random coexistence. Does purpose exist or is it merely another concept we created?

When we look at nature and the fine precision with which it is built, we can't help but wonder that something with so much finesse couldn't possibly be random. The food chain, for example, has such intricate interconnectivity that removing anything out of it disrupts its entire balance. Evolution, for that matter, happened with such precision that the odds of it happening in the manner that it did are extreme. Surely, nature happens to be in perfection and such perfection definitely must have a reason behind it. At least that is what one is compelled to believe.

We are simply nature, experiencing and understanding itself. The human mind is merely a tool to witness this beautiful journey of nature's evolution. With the development of the human mind, nature has finally reached the point where it can experience itself and understand what it is all about. Our existence holds a very cosmic significance and it goes beyond our daily lives and duties that we so strongly like to hold on to. Our routine, requires at least a few moments, to let this fact sink in before we begin to chase money or understand how much it really matters in the larger scheme of events.

We need survival and a homemaker needs to take care of her house, but it is not her purpose, is something that she needs to be aware of at least once in a day. In the same way, the man who needs to provide for his family, needs to realise that as much as the financial well being of his family is important, it is still not his purpose in life. They both need to remind themselves that they are a part of nature's journey of self awareness. It is all around us when we really think about it.

When we look at trees, plants and other animals, we surely ought to remind ourselves about how we are connected on a cosmic scale and to feel that connection is something that brings us closer to true purpose. When we are aware of who we are, it is a direct link to the whole of nature and when we silently feel that connection then our worries about our life, in general, gradually begin to fade into the minuteness of their existence.

This clarity of purpose is a tool that can help us get through all the stress that worries us daily and it lies in cherishing all the little things. This mind that is capable of such awareness surely needs to be cherished once in a while too. The joy of the connectivity with nature can be found in the wetness of the green grass or the chirping of the birds if you find the time for it. When the mind realises itself and its ability to cherish all this, then It comes to the final realization that there is nothing to be worried about at all because the present moment has all the beauty of fulfilling nature's purpose of existence. When you realise where you are in regard with nature and how deeply you are connected, you reach self awareness and all your problems appear smaller and fixable. Nature's purpose was to experience and understand itself and once you align with that purpose, then not only does it give you the strength to face anything but also tells you how little your worries mean and how, most of the times, they don't even matter.

□

## *Chapter 12*
# Singularity

We, as humans, are unlike any other species. Every one of us is different and has a different set of desires and tastes. We behave differently with different people and to be able to choose who we are or how exactly we define ourselves then becomes the question. To attain a sense of singularity with our being is often not easy. We are looking for that perfect self image that we can project but that never comes to us easily.

Now, there are people who would like to relieve stress by going into a club with their friends and at the same time there are people who would rather sit at a coffee house and discuss a book over a simple cup of coffee. Neither can you expect the people from the coffee house to enjoy their time with a loud and chirpy group at the club nor can you expect the people from the club to enjoy a boring evening at a coffee house. They are both critical of each other. They have both already chosen their self image to a certain extent and that is what makes them rigid and critical of each other's choices.

Despite choosing a persona we often find ourselves on the opposite side of the spectrum. So is to say, that if you are, say, a great orator or a teacher who is often surrounded by listeners, then there will also be times when you become a listener among a group of scholars where you are not a popular orator.

Your persona or how you define yourself cannot always be imposed on a situation. Say, when you are among your school friends who have always considered you as the humourous joker of the group, you have to step out of your definition of yourself and play that role. You may consider yourself as a person who would have sincere and serious intellectual conversations with your new friends but when you are with your old friends, they have an image of you that is already well designed and their perception of you is what they have kept alive. You will be a complete stranger to them if you do not play the role in which they have always seen you. You may not even feel like making a joke but for them to consider taking you seriously is a very farfetched notion.

This shift in behaviour happens when you begin to question who you really are and the idea of projecting an older version of yourself seems tedious and unnecessary. However, what has happened here is that circumstance has created a vessel within which you are supposed to fit in. The rigidity of your new persona is unable to take shape in this vessel. What we need to understand is that, in terms of circumstance, sometimes you are the teacher and sometimes you are the student and the imposition of your persona is not possible in every circumstance.

It should not worry you because it is not that you have lost the sense of who you are in that situation, but rather you are not used to the complexity of the vessel around you.

So, when you are stuck at the club with loud people then you can either feel that you are stuck and have a horrible evening or you can learn to take every moment in with grace. Your persona cannot fit in to every vessel and therefore there are times when you have to be the vessel itself. When you are in the club then, you are the club and you have to align your frequency to the vessel of this circumstance.

Being the vessel is when multiple personalities of a person coexist within that vessel and are projected when required. Say, when you are at the coffee house having a peaceful discussion about a book with a friend then you have to ensure that you understand that even if you enjoy this version of yourself, it is still not who you really are. You have to remain somewhat detached from this version of yourself. Your personality has vast potential and cannot be rigidly summarised into singularity. This is to say, that you can still have a good time dancing your heart out at the club and not miss the coffee shop.

Whoever we are in a moment is certainly defined by the circumstance of that time. To be in alignment with nature is what makes a wholesome person. There is a part of you that is the hilarious joker to your school friends and there is also a part of you that would rather discuss a book. This duality of your being is what makes you a complete personality.

Every situation builds a vessel for you to fit in to

and you need not be disheartened when the vessel is not of your liking. Instead you have to be that vessel knowing that it is temporary and does not define you. So, say that even if you are a joker to your friends, a teacher to your colleagues, you are still only a patient to your therapist. His projection of you is the vessel he designed to portray you in a different light and when you become the vessel, then you know that whatever shape your personality takes in that moment, is not who you really are but rather a mere temporary illusion of who you are. Unless he makes an effort to get to know you completely, he can only make an assumption of who you are. So to choose to be the vessel means to stay calm and let versions of your personalities step in and out depending on the circumstance you are placed in. To accept yourself as a mere vessel of nature where persona is fluid and a temporary presence, is when you attain oneness with nature. The singularity then always remains alive despite the contradictions of the self.

Once you have attained this oneness you would soon realise that you are less worried about how people see you and your conflict with trying to attain a true self has been erased. Even when our self is not perfectly projected, it still remains and nature and circumstance stops having an impact on our perception of our selves. We now know who we really are and the urge to project our persona on every situation fades. It is a more mature understanding of our self.

This is when you can finally have a joyous night at the club and still enjoy a peaceful cup of coffee.

You can have a serious discussion and still be a humourous man to your friends. You remain lively and dissolve into every situation with ease. The chase for singularity is addictive and arises out of a desperate need to cast an impression on people. When you begin to think beyond how you might appear to a person is when you're truly free to be yourself.

The truth is that you can only be a teacher when a genuine and calm listener is present. His aura is what defines your vessel. People and circumstances have a huge impact on who we become in a particular scenario. So in a certain sense, you might not be a joker but the people around you, can make you one. You might not even be the person who likes having intellectual discourses on books at a coffee shop, but the person with you, can make you that person. You are never out to sell your image, in fact, you don't even have one. You always are merely the vessel through which your personality floats. It differs depending on the circumstance you are in. So when you feel like you did not like the way you were projected in a particular scenario then you should remember that it was never up to you in the first place. Your circumstances and the people around you define who you appear to be and who you are in reality is irrelevant in that sense. If there is a time where you are not projected as per your expectations then there will always also be a time when your projection exceeded your expectations.

It is not your job to impress people all the time and your impression is majorly dependent on how they wished to perceive you as well. So it never makes sense to be disheartened by say, an interview that went bad or a woman that did not like you. What you've got to know is that there is no perfect 'you' that fits into every vessel that circumstance designs for you. You can only truly know that when you become the vessel itself and understand its limits that correspond to your shape. You have to dissolve into it and attain oneness with its nature. You will then be in oneness with nature itself and in time you will find your place as long as you stop chasing your urge to attain singularity in terms of persona.

□

## *Chapter 13*

# Satisfaction

We are all caught up in a web of desires where we are constantly longing for more and we spend our entire lives acquiring more and more. It is also true that our social standing also depends on that and we feel the need to impress people around us by acquiring more wealth. Society as well, expects you to constantly work harder to achieve more and that is how they measure your success. As a provider for the household it is also expected that you provide your family with all the luxuries that they need. So, in a certain sense, there is also an inherent pressure from the world outside that pushes you running for desires. The fact is no matter how much wealth you acquire in your journey you are never completely satisfied. There is a new want waiting for us even before we begin to enjoy the fruits of our labour.

A man who rides a bike needs a car and the one with a car needs a bigger car. We all regularly go to work in the hope of earning a better payout and if in case we do get one, we are still looking for a payout that is more than the one we now have. The ultimate goal behind all these endeavours is to attain satisfaction. However, we never reach that point of supreme satisfaction where we stop wanting more. There are monks and saints that give up all worldly desires and live within the bare minimum requirements. They are looking for satisfaction as well. They do not feel the urge to look for anything more than what they have but there is still something that constantly pulls us away from feeling truly satisfied.

The problem with the human mind is that it is constantly flooded with thoughts and a state of complete thoughtlessness is what we really need. The whole idea of meditation is built around attaining thoughtlessness. It teaches us to be able to focus our minds in a way where we are conscious of every thought and we learn to let it go. When we learn to let thoughts go is when we are at peace. This stability or peace comes from embracing the silence and feeling the present moment in its fullness.

Now, we as humans, either live in the past or in the future. Every thought you will find among this flood will be either a regret of the past or a worry about the future. Your mind is disjointed from reality in this sense. Every moment, potentially, can be a moment of satisfaction but we are so caught up in the material world that we can never feel satisfied with anything that we achieve. Even when we do feel satisfied it is short-lived. We move on too quickly. We find ourselves rushing for a new want and anything that we achieved previously begins to lose value.

Though practicing detachment or serious meditation can bring you closer to feeling satisfied, as you gradually learn to give up pleasure and become thoughtless, there will still be moments of emptiness that you would find. Meditation as a practice is a perfect way to attain thoughtlessness and channelise your energies and can even momentarily bring you closer to peace. You could force yourself to practice detachment where you learn to be satisfied with what you have. The question then is does that truly make you satisfied when you are in contradiction with satisfaction itself?

There is no doubt that the satisfaction you feel when you are at peace is the closest you can get to feeling complete but what after that? You couldn't possibly sit silently forever. Moreover as long as you are a member of the society everyone around you would expect you to contribute to the world outside and from a pragmatic point of view, it is not possible for you to renounce everything and be at peace forever. Let us say, you even manage to convince your family to let you practice detachment and meditation, would you be able to survive without doing anything? At the same time the society around you will also feel that you don't do anything and your social standing will suffer and you would be considered crazy at best. Would you be able to live with that image of yourself? We are always conscious of what people think about us and acknowledgement from people around us is something that we constantly seek. Would you be able to live without that acknowledgement from people around you?

So, How do we really attain satisfaction in a practical scenario?

Firstly, the idea of meditation is to attain thoughtlessness and to be able to feel the present moment for what it is and attain stability of mind. Secondly, the idea of detachment is a little different from its traditional understanding too. We are not discarding these ideas at all. A sense of detachment is actually about not being attached to what you have but that does not mean that you don't need to have anything. Essentially it means that you have what you have but you can live without it. You have to have a detached approach to life. It essentially means that you are letting things happen rather than chasing after them. That is to say that you are now not looking for a better payout but you are open to the idea of having one. You do not have to give up on your desires but you are supposed to conquer them.

Detachment is a certain sense of indifference towards worldly possessions where you become the observer of your own life passing through you. You accept what life gives you and at the same time you never chase after what you want. Instead you begin to examine what you want and why you feel the need to want it. Eventually you conquer this want to the point that you feel sufficient without it as well.

The most important factor apart from detachment, thoughtlessness and peace is the idea of feeling the moment and enjoying the little joys. The idea is that when you have a thoughtless, detached and stable peaceful mind then you would not be thinking of buying a car while walking barefoot on green grass rather you would feel the pleasure of walking on green grass and the joy it brings. You need to accept that the future is uncertain and maybe you will never be able to buy a car at all and still feel the joy that the green grass brings to you. In this way you get to feel the satisfaction that the grass has to offer you even when life is not moving in the way you would have desired. The satisfaction from the grass then becomes so overwhelming that you could have just been fired from your job and would still have a smile on your face while walking on the grass.

The idea is to give utmost importance to the grass that exists within the present moment and the breeze that flows along with it. It is to not be bothered by regrets of why you were fired and what could have been done differently and at the same time not be worried about how you are going to find another job. The idea is to let things happen with their natural flow and to smoothly sail over it by always being in the present moment.

Such an understanding seems absurd but can be attained once we gradually realise what is important in which moment. Moreover, the ultimate goal of life was always to attain satisfaction and achieving it can become easier when we learn to shift our perspective rather than chasing after things. Satisfaction can only be achieved within the 'here and now' of things. So, if you are worried about your future then as reasonable as it seems, it is taking away the satisfaction of the present moment. Which is why a thoughtless and stable mind is required to deal with overwhelming worries of the future.

Finally, a sense of detachment is what helps in the shifting of perspective. When you are indifferent to what has happened or is about to happen is when you move through life with a confidence that is unwavering. Which is to say that getting fired from your job does not matter to you in the least because you were never too attached to it to begin with. At the same time since your needs and wants are limited, you are satisfied with whatever job life brings you to and you would let things happen rather than trying to force them in a certain direction. So, now, you are not waiting for the satisfaction of getting a new job but rather you are already satisfied before getting one.

Detachment brings perspective, thoughtlessness brings stability and the ability to be in the present moment and find the little joys brings eternal satisfaction. The fact is that we were always looking for satisfaction in the wrong places and the paradox is that it can only truly be found once you stop chasing after it.

□

## *Chapter 14*
# Curiosity

In this day and age, we as humans have reached a point where we almost know everything that is necessary for survival. In fact we know much more than that. The science behind how plants operate or the chemistry behind the medicines we need or be it the technology at our fingertips, we have truly excelled in terms of knowledge and we can owe it all to curiosity. Everything is accessible and all the knowledge you could imagine is available for free on the internet. All of this has been possible due to the curiosity of the human mind.

A thinker is burdened with this curiosity and he never settles till he knows all that there is to know about his particular passion. Curiosity in fact develops passion. The options in terms of profession are endless and finding our passion is dependent on what makes us curious. We are all collectively working towards knowing more and more and the quest for knowledge, we have realised over time, is a never ending one because there is always something more to know and we still haven't found all the answers to this vast universe.

However, we could safely say that we know enough to survive and live in luxury to a certain extent. Moreover since a thinker is cursed with curiosity, there will always be people that are searching for more answers in terms of science. Governments and private enterprises will continue funding more scientific enquiries and we will only move forward in terms of knowledge. The amount of knowledge needed to spend a decent life is finally here due to the centuries of struggle and it is all owed to curiosity.

There are so many fields of knowledge that even if we spend our entire lives studiously we couldn't possibly know everything. Let us say that if we do reach the end of the line and collectively end up knowing everything that there is to know as humans, what then would be our next step? The question then is, what happens after all curiosity ends?

Will we all be at peace with our lives and will we be content? More importantly, do we need to wait for all the answers to the universe to find contentment in our lives?

Though it is true that the curious thinker seeks contentment in his quest for more knowledge, his curiosity is what fuels his feelings and he feels satisfied when he learns something new. He is in a certain sense burdened with the curse of curiosity and he will never settle till he possibly knows all that there is to know. He is not wrong in pursuing knowledge at any step. However, there are dimensions to life that he is missing out on, that he is completely unaware of. He is so immersed in his pursuit that he is unable to take in the joy the present moment already brings with itself.

Let us say, there is a man who works at a tea stall. He works tirelessly in a day to make ends meet. He knows that he makes the best tea and there is a decent turnout at his tea stall everyday. He goes home content with his day's work everyday. He does not feel the need to be curious about any other knowledge besides how to make the best tea. Making tea is his passion and he is great at it.

What then differentiates everyone else from that man at the tea stall?

The truth is that we look down on humble professions and in our quest for social mobility we think that making tea isn't something worth being curious about. Apart from our curiosity about our professions we also need a social standing and want to be known for something. We need the luxuries of life to maintain our standard of living and we make choices around our social stature. We feel that working at that tea stall is beneath us. In our quest for the so called 'knowledge' we end up losing out on contentment and peace which the man at the tea stall has. We burden our minds with books and all kinds of philosophies to reach the zenith of knowledge in our fields and still end up never being truly content.

Being curious and never being at peace is always considered a virtue and the idea of hustling, reaching for more and working hard is praised all around the world. We never realise that our curiosity becomes our enemy because it takes away from us true pleasure, peace and contentment.

There is nothing wrong in aiming big and making it big but at the same time the thing to wonder is that is not everything we do to attain social stability, at the end of the day merely a profession.

Our energies and curiosities could be channelised when we take genuine interest in someone else's life, when we feel connected with them and share a real emotional bond, when we meet new people with the intention of truly feeling connected with the universe around us while still humbly working at a tea stall.

The tea stall analogy is meant just to shed light on the fact that our profession and our quest for knowledge and answers, is a quest that when one fully immerses into, loses out on the real joy of life. Life is too short to always remain curious and dedicate entirely to some greater human quest. More importantly the universe is vast and we may never know all the answers to it even if we spend our entire lives searching for them.

Intellectualism is a disease and those who suffer from it can never rest until they possibly know all that there is to know in their thirst for enquiry. At the end of the line peace and contentment awaits us all and it is never too late to feel it before the world has all the answers. Curiosity is a simultaneous journey and your quest for answers should never overwhelm you completely.

Moreover, the joy of life hides in the humblest of professions and the little things that give you joy and racing for something with all your heart will never fulfill you even after achieving all the success in your field. One needs to be at peace with the life he has now before he can imagine a better tomorrow.

To contribute to something greater is not wrong but it isn't the only thing that suffices. If you lose out on living while you are running for your goals then the achievement of your goals will never be fulfilling.

It is understandable that there are people who are thinkers and are burdened which such quests while at the same time there are other beings that live for the moment. There is nothing wrong with being either of them but living life is more than just the knowledge you can acquire in this short span.

We need to essentially understand the difference between information and true knowledge. Most of what we think is knowledge is actually just information about a particular field. Say, the field of medicine, all that we know and understand about it is mere information and our curiosity towards it is not a wrong one to have but it still cannot be considered as knowledge. True knowledge lies in understanding what life is really about and how to live it. True knowledge lies in attaining contentment and peace with what you already have. It lies in places that you have always looked down upon.

The life of the man working at a tea stall is not any less complete than yours. In fact he lives beyond ambition and dreams and in a certain sense, understands life a little better than you do because while you are busy chasing your dreams, he is living life to the fullest and is probably happier than you ever will be.

When we begin to imagine beyond dreams and ambition is when we realise the true meaning of life. After all we are all like children that are contemplating occupation throughout our lives and in this blindness of a social standing we neither get completely attached to other humans and we don't find peace either. Our times have enough information to finally take a step into the domain of peace and contentment. Our curiosity should be for other humans. Our curiosity should be towards finding peace. Our curiosity should be about real communication and connectivity with the people around us. We have already reached so far in terms of science that we need to take a step back and explore dimensions to life that we missed out on collectively, as a society.

Our chase needs to end and we need to give time to ourselves and people around us. When we begin to do that we realise that our dreams are not far away from being fulfilled and all that we were never curious about gives us a completion that we never imagined. We can all collectively move towards the technologically advanced society that we are aiming for while still being content with where we are now, because it is the most beautiful time to live in as it is. It does not need a chase that earlier generations desperately needed. Information can always be chased but it is life that is fleeting away from us and in our curiosity we might just end up missing out on what mattered most. A better collective future is what we all dream of and it can only be achieved by a society that lives in contentment with what it already has. There is an ocean of life worth living around you and when you take the little joys along with your curiosity towards your quest, only then will you find that your journey was worth it.

□

## *Chapter 15*

# Closure

Every book, film or art form demands an ending note. A passage that finally gives us a sense of closure. A certain point where things conclude and take a shape. It is not in the author's mind to give that shape because creativity keeps on longing for more and the author could possibly go on, but he needs to fit inside a structure. A structure that is the demand of his intended audience. As viewers and readers we long for that place where we can gain closure and move on.

As newer art forms have flourished, we see artists trying to experiment with shape and often leave their artwork on cliffhangers. They tend to make their art readerly and leave it unto their audience to fill in the gaps and make do with their own sense of closure. It is certainly an experimental approach and an attempt on the artist's part to break through the structure. However, even cliffhangers give the audience a certain sense of closure. It leaves you at a place where you use your mind to draw your own conclusion. It leaves you in a place where you could move on.

There must have been times in our lives where

we would have read a book halfway through and then left it as it is. There must have been films too that you watch halfway and leave it at that. Even those half read books and unwatched films are never left at a point where we are longing for more. We never leave at a point where our curiosity for closure has not been satiated. So in that sense we have still found our closure with it and we can move on to the next thing.

The need for closure is an inherent part of our being and we definitely do find ways to get it one way or another. It is actually a part of the structure we are bound to see things in. As an artist it is very hard to break through that structure and paint outside the lines. Every artist longs to give their audience something that is lasting and hard to move on from. The artist wants his art to be eternal and something that can always be revisited. The artist wants this not only for glory, but to create something that satiates the thirst of his intended audience indefinitely. He wants to create something that is beyond structure and an endless joy for his audience.

The idea here is to create that endless essence that breaks all structures and paints way outside the lines. The endlessness that can be found within the universe inside of us and the vast expanse outside. An essence that gives you relief and confidence every time you read through it.

As a final piece, we need the ability to look beyond closure. We need the ability to break through the structure in which life takes shape. Our curiosity for a closure needs an end. We need to go deeper and find stillness and peace with something that is endless.

We need to develop in ourselves the ability to cherish the stillness and silence of this universe.

We need to be able to stay still, calm and feel the silence that we have developed within our thoughts. We need to value the fact that we exist. We need to be able to stare into the endlessness of the universe that surrounds us and fill our minds with a silent nothingness. Once we have that, we can gradually realise that we exist in this universe as observers and we can find peace in that. The stability of our minds is now at its peak and we feel nothing but an endless peace of pure existence. As we observe only our breath and slowly observe everything around, we feel nothing apart from that peace. We are at a point where the social structures that we have created can be seen for what they are.

Our worries have now taken a back seat and the intention here is to give you that same sense of stability and peace every time you feel that you cannot feel it anymore. Collectively we break through the structure and instead of leaving you at a pretentious cliffhanger or a closing piece, we have now completed a cycle that breaks through its structure and takes you towards the soundness of your peaceful mind.

This journey is a constant one and you need to step into your 'self' everyday to simply feel the joy of your own existence. The fact that you are present to witness the beauty of the vast nature around you and the ability to find peace with feeling oneness with it, is an endless endeavour.

There will be days when you feel that it is not enough and you will either be longing for something to do or someone to meet. You will have days when you would look for worldly pleasures as well. There will always be time for all of that and there is nothing wrong in looking to fulfill your desires but as and when you come closer to this soundness of mind everyday, you will realise that it is all you really need to put your worries aside and you would stop feeling the urge to move on from it. It is something that works in a fascinating way and breaks the structure of living a life that has been defined into a shape. You will learn to paint outside the lines and find this endless joy as something that does not need closure. It is a pure feeling that works beyond your curiosities and your urge to move on.

The silence and stillness will then be an essential part of you. It will become something that you do not feel the urge to let go and move on to the next thing from. A reading of this piece should not be anything less than a way of life and the intention here is to give you something that lasts. A revisit should be able to energize you and channelise your energies into a whole again every time you feel that the worries of this world our getting to you. As you make this a part of your life you will know that your path is one of oneness with nature and you are slowly becoming complete.

As you step into this domain, you gradually realise that all these social structures like schooling or your job are mere constructs that we have created to give meaning to our lives. They have been created so that we can distract our minds with something as we age. These are mere structures that we use to define ourselves as people that function within a society. You are now already beyond society and its expectations from you. You don't need to centre yourself around these structures that society has imposed on you. When you step into this new domain, you will realise that these are structures that you don't need at all as you have found inner peace in the endless river of serenity that your mind now is.

This piece hopes that it can be that essential part of your life that can always be revisited for rejuvenation of your energies and the rewiring of your brain. It hopes to give you the objective viewpoint that we are living lives in structures and we do not have to hold on to them as we go along, for they are not the essence of our lives and after all are mere distractions to engage our time in.

It often happens when we are playing a game, we end up getting too serious about it and forget that after all, it is only a game. We need to merely practice this sense of detachment from life long enough to understand that it is not very different from any other game except that we have immersed deeply into it and are a little too seriously invested in it. When we learn to be one with the universe around us we realise that this investment is all for no real reason and is merely noise from 'the matrix' that we have failed to ignore. When we see this noise for what it is, we can begin to live up to the full potential of a human mind. We are unconquerable in our essence and we need to let go of the fear of losing in our lives because after all, even this life is merely an immersive and highly overrated game and it is absolutely pointless to take it too seriously.

□□□